East o' the Sun and West o' the Moon

and Other Norwegian Fairy Tales

East o' the Sun and West o' the Moon

and Other Norwegian Fairy Tales

GEORGE WEBBE DASENT

DOVER PUBLICATIONS, INC.
Mineola, New York

DOVER JUVENILE CLASSICS
EDITOR OF THIS VOLUME: ELAINE WILL SPARBER

Copyright

Copyright © 2001 by Dover Publications, Inc.
All rights reserved under Pan American and International Copyright Conventions.

Published in Canada by General Publishing Company, Ltd., 30 Lesmill Road, Don Mills, Toronto, Ontario.

Bibliographical Note

This Dover edition, first published in 2001, is a new selection of stories reprinted from the third edition of the work published by David Douglas, Edinburgh, in 1888 under the title *Popular Tales from the Norse*.

Library of Congress Cataloging-in-Publication Data

Asbjørnsen, Peter Christen, 1812–1885.
    [Norske folke-eventyr. English Selections]
    East o' the sun and west o' the moon and other Norwegian fairy tales / [translated by] George Webbe Dasent.
       p.   cm. — (Dover juvenile classics)
    "A republication of selected stories by Peter Christen Asbjørnsen and Jørgen Moe in Popular tales from the Norse" . . . T.p. verso.
    Contents: East o' the sun and west o' the moon — Why the sea is salt — Twelve wild ducks — Mastermaid — Boots who made the Princess say, "That's a story" — Dapplegrim — Tatterhood — Soria Moria Castle — Princess on the Glass Hill — Shortshanks.
    ISBN 0-486-41724-7 (pbk.)
    1. Fairy tales—Norway. 2. Tales—Norway. [1. Fairy tales. 2. Folklore—Norway.] I. Moe, Jørgen Engebretsen, 1813–1882. II. Dasent, George Webbe, Sir, 1817–1896. III. Title. IV. Series.

PZ8.D19 Eas   2001
398.2'09481—dc21

00–052300

Manufactured in the United States of America
Dover Publications, Inc., 31 East 2nd Street, Mineola, N.Y. 11501

Contents

East o' the Sun and West o' the Moon
and Other Norwegian
Fairy Tales

East o' the Sun and West o' the Moon

ONCE ON a time there was a poor farmer who had so many children that he hadn't much of either food or clothing to give them. Pretty children they all were, but the prettiest was the youngest daughter, who was so lovely there was no end to her loveliness.

So one day, 'twas on a Thursday evening late at the fall of the year, the weather was so wild and rough outside, and it was so cruelly dark, and rain fell and wind blew, till the walls of the cottage shook again. There they all sat round the fire busy with this thing and that. But just then, all at once something gave three taps on the window-pane. Then the father went out to see what was the matter; and, when he got out of doors, what should he see but a great big White Bear.

"Good evening to you," said the White Bear.

"The same to you," said the man.

"Will you give me your youngest daughter? If you will, I'll make you as rich as you are now poor," said the Bear.

Well, the man would not be at all sorry to be so rich; but still he thought he must have a bit of a talk with his daughter first; so he went in and told them how there was a great White Bear waiting outside, who had given his word to make them so rich if he could only have the youngest daughter.

The lassie said "No!" outright. Nothing could get her to say anything else; so the man went out and settled it with

1

the White Bear, that he should come again the next Thursday evening and get an answer. Meantime he talked his daughter over, and kept on telling her of all the riches they would get, and how well off she would be herself; and so at last she thought better of it, and washed and mended her rags, made herself as smart as she could, and was ready to start. I can't say her packing gave her much trouble.

Next Thursday evening came the White Bear to fetch her, and she got upon his back with her bundle, and off they went. So, when they had gone a bit of the way, the White Bear said—

"Are you afraid?"

"No! she wasn't."

"Well! mind and hold tight by my shaggy coat, and then there's nothing to fear," said the Bear.

So she rode a long, long way, till they came to a great steep hill. There, on the face of it, the White Bear gave a knock, and a door opened, and they came into a castle, where there were many rooms all lit up; rooms gleaming with silver and gold; and there too was a table ready laid, and it was all as grand as grand could be. Then the White Bear gave her a silver bell; and when she wanted anything, she was only to ring it, and she would get it at once.

Well, after she had eaten and drunk, and evening wore on, she got sleepy after her journey, and thought she would like to go to bed, so she rang the bell; and she had scarce taken hold of it before she came into a chamber, where there was a bed made, as fair and white as any one would wish to sleep in, with silken pillows and curtains, and gold fringe. All that was in the room was gold or silver; but when she had gone to bed, and put out the light, a man came and laid himself alongside of her. That was the White Bear, who threw off his beast shape at night; but she never saw him, for he always came after she had put out the light, and before the day dawned he was up and off again. So things went on happily for a while, but at last she began to get silent and sorrowful; for there she went about all day alone, and she longed to go home to see her father and mother, and brothers and sisters. So one day, when the White Bear asked what it was that she lacked, she said it was so dull and lonely there, and how she longed to go home to see her father and mother, and brothers and sisters, and that was why she was so sad and sorrowful, because she couldn't get to them.

"Well, well!" said the Bear, "perhaps there's a cure for all this; but you must promise me one thing, not to talk alone with your mother, but only when the rest are by to hear; for she'll take you by the hand and try to lead you into a room alone to talk; but you must mind and not do that, else you'll bring bad luck on both of us."

So one Sunday the White Bear came and said now they could set off to see her father and mother. Well, off they started, she sitting on his back; and they went far and long. At last they came to a grand house, and there her brothers and sisters were running about out of doors at play, and everything was so pretty, 'twas a joy to see.

"This is where your father and mother live now," said the White Bear; "but don't forget what I told you, else you'll make us both unlucky."

"No! bless her, she'd not forget"; and when she had reached the house, the White Bear turned right about and left her.

Then when she went in to see her father and mother, there was such joy, there was no end to it. None of them thought they could thank her enough for all she had done for them. Now, they had everything they wished, as good as good could be, and they all wanted to know how she got on where she lived.

Well, she said, it was very good to live where she did; she had all she wished. What she said beside I don't know; but I don't think any of them had the right end of the stick, or that they got much out of her. But so in the afternoon, after they had done dinner, all happened as the White

Bear had said. Her mother wanted to talk with her alone in her bed-room; but she minded what the White Bear had said, and wouldn't go up stairs.

"Oh, what we have to talk about will keep," she said, and put her mother off. But somehow or other, her mother got round her at last, and she had to tell her the whole story. So she said, how every night, when she had gone to bed, a man came and lay down beside her as soon as she had put out the light, and how she never saw him, because he was always up and away before the morning dawned; and how she went about woeful and sorrowing, for she thought she should so like to see him, and how all day long she walked about there alone, and how dull, and dreary, and lonesome it was.

"My!" said her mother; "it may well be a Troll you slept with! But now I'll teach you a lesson how to set eyes on him. I'll give you a bit of candle, which you can carry home in your bosom; just light that while he is asleep, but take care not to drip the wax on him."

Yes! she took the candle, and hid it in her bosom, and as night drew on, the White Bear came and fetched her away.

But when they had gone a bit of the way, the White Bear asked if all hadn't happened as he had said.

"Well, she couldn't say it hadn't."

"Now, mind," said he, "if you have listened to your mother's advice, you have brought bad luck on us both, and then, all that has passed between us will be as nothing."

"No," she said, "she hadn't listened to her mother's advice."

So when she reached home, and had gone to bed, it was the old story over again. There came a man and lay down beside her; but at dead of night, when she heard he slept, she got up and struck a light, lit the candle, and let the light shine on him, and so she saw that he was the loveliest Prince one ever set eyes on, and she fell so deep in love with him on the spot, that she thought she couldn't live if she didn't give him a kiss there and then. And so she did, but as she kissed him, she dripped three hot drops of wax on his shirt, and he woke up.

"What have you done?" he cried; "now you have made us both unlucky, for had you held out only this one year, I had been freed. For I have a stepmother who has bewitched me, so that I am a White Bear by day, and a Man by night. But now all ties are snapt between us; now I must set off from you to her. She lives in a castle which stands EAST O' THE SUN AND WEST O' THE MOON, and there, too, is a Princess, with a nose three yards long, and she's the wife I must have now."

She wept and took it ill, but there was no help for it; go he must.

Then she asked if she mightn't go with him.

No, she mightn't.

"Tell me the way, then," she said, "and I'll search you out; *that* surely I may get leave to do."

"Yes, she might do that," he said; "but there was no way to that place. It lay EAST O' THE SUN AND WEST O' THE MOON, and thither she'd never find her way."

So next morning, when she woke up, both Prince and castle were gone, and then she lay on a little green patch, in the midst of the gloomy thick wood, and by her side lay the same bundle of rags she had brought with her from her old home.

So when she had rubbed the sleep out of her eyes, and wept till she was tired, she set out on her way, and walked many, many days, till she came to a lofty crag. Under it sat an old hag, and played with a gold apple which she tossed about. Her the lassie asked if she knew the way to the Prince, who lived with his stepmother in the castle that lay EAST O' THE SUN AND WEST O' THE MOON, and who was to marry the Princess with a nose three yards long.

"How did you come to know about him?" asked the old hag; "but maybe you are the lassie who ought to have had him?"

Yes, she was.

"So, so; it's you, is it?" said the old hag. "Well, all I know

about him is, that he lives in the castle that lies EAST O' THE
SUN AND WEST O' THE MOON, and thither you'll come, late or
never; but still you may have the loan of my horse, and on
him you can ride to my next neighbour. Maybe she'll be
able to tell you; and when you get there, just give the
horse a switch under the left ear, and beg him to be off
home; and, stay, this gold apple you may take with you."

So she got upon the horse, and rode a long long time,
till she came to another crag, under which sat another old
hag, with a gold carding-comb. Her the lassie asked if she
knew the way to the castle that lay EAST O' THE SUN AND
WEST O' THE MOON, and she answered, like the first old hag,
that she knew nothing about it, except it was east o' the
sun and west o' the moon.

"And thither you'll come, late or never; but you shall
have the loan of my horse to my next neighbour; maybe
she'll tell you all about it; and when you get there, just
switch the horse under the left ear, and beg him to be
off home."

And this old hag gave her the golden carding-comb;
it might be she'd find some use for it, she said. So the
lassie got up on the horse, and rode a far far way, and a
weary time; and so at last she came to another great crag,
under which sat another old hag, spinning with a golden
spinning-wheel. Her, too, she asked if she knew the way
to the Prince, and where the castle was that lay EAST O'
THE SUN AND WEST O' THE MOON. So it was the same thing
over again.

"Maybe it's you who ought to have had the Prince?"
said the old hag.

Yes, it was.

But she, too, didn't know the way a bit better than the
other two. "East o' the sun and west o' the moon it was,"
she knew—that was all.

"And thither you'll come, late or never; but I'll lend you
my horse, and then I think you'd best ride to the East
Wind and ask him; maybe he knows those parts, and can
blow you thither. But when you get to him, you need only

give the horse a switch under the left ear, and he'll trot home of himself."

And so, too, she gave her the gold spinning-wheel. "Maybe you'll find a use for it," said the old hag.

Then on she rode many many days, a weary time, before she got to the East Wind's house, but at last she did reach it, and then she asked the East Wind if he could tell her the way to the Prince who dwelt east o' the sun and west o' the moon. Yes, the East Wind had often heard tell of it, the Prince and the castle, but he couldn't tell the way, for he had never blown so far.

"But, if you will, I'll go with you to my brother the West Wind, maybe he knows, for he's much stronger. So, if you will just get on my back, I'll carry you thither."

Yes, she got on his back, and I should just think they went briskly along.

So when they got there, they went into the West Wind's house, and the East Wind said the lassie he had brought was the one who ought to have had the Prince who lived in the castle EAST O' THE SUN AND WEST O' THE MOON; and so she had set out to seek him, and how he had come with her, and would be glad to know if the West Wind knew how to get to the castle.

"Nay," said the West Wind, "so far I've never blown; but if you will, I'll go with you to our brother the South Wind, for he's much stronger than either of us, and he has flapped his wings far and wide. Maybe he'll tell you. You can get on my back, and I'll carry you to him."

Yes! she got on his back, and so they travelled to the South Wind, and weren't so very long on the way, I should think.

When they got there, the West Wind asked him if he could tell her the way to the castle that lay EAST O' THE SUN AND WEST O' THE MOON, for it was she who ought to have had the Prince who lived there.

"You don't say so! That's she, is it?" said the South Wind.

"Well, I have blustered about in most places in my time, but so far have I never blown; but if you will, I'll take you to my brother the North Wind; he is the oldest and strongest of the whole lot of us, and if he don't know where it is, you'll never find any one in the world to tell you. You can get on my back, and I'll carry you thither."

Yes! she got on his back, and away he went from his house at a fine rate. And this time, too, she wasn't long on her way.

So when they got to the North Wind's house, he was so wild and cross, cold puffs came from him a long way off.

"BLAST YOU BOTH, WHAT DO YOU WANT?" he roared out to them ever so far off, so that it struck them with an icy shiver.

"Well," said the South Wind, "you needn't be so foul-mouthed, for here I am, your brother, the South Wind, and here is the lassie who ought to have had the Prince who dwells in the castle that lies EAST O' THE SUN AND WEST O' THE MOON, and now she wants to ask you if you ever were there, and can tell her the way, for she would be so glad to find him again."

"YES, I KNOW WELL ENOUGH WHERE IT IS," said the North Wind; "once in my life I blew an aspen-leaf thither, but I was so tired I couldn't blow a puff for ever so many days after. But if you really wish to go thither, and aren't afraid to come along with me, I'll take you on my back and see if I can blow you thither."

Yes! with all her heart; she must and would get thither if it were possible in any way; and as for fear, however madly he went, she wouldn't be at all afraid.

"Very well, then," said the North Wind, "But you must sleep here to-night, for we must have the whole day before us, if we're to get thither at all."

Early next morning the North Wind woke her, and puffed himself up, and blew himself out, and made himself so stout and big, 'twas gruesome to look at him; and so off they went high up through the air, as if they would never stop till they got to the world's end.

Down here below there was such a storm; it threw

down long tracts of wood and many houses, and when it swept over the great sea, ships sank by the hundreds.

So they tore on and on—no one can believe how far they went—and all the while they still went over the sea, and the North Wind got more and more weary, and so out of breath he could scarce bring out a puff, and his wings drooped and drooped, till at last he sunk so low that the crests of the waves dashed over his heels.

"Are you afraid?" said the North Wind.

"No!" she wasn't.

But they weren't very far from land; and the North Wind had still so much strength left in him that he managed to throw her up on the shore under the windows of the castle which lay EAST O' THE SUN AND WEST O' THE MOON; but then he was so weak and worn out, he had to stay there and rest many days before he could get home again.

Next morning the lassie sat down under the castle window, and began to play with the gold apple; and the first person she saw was the Long-nose who was to have the Prince.

"What do you want for your gold apple, you lassie?" said the Long-nose, and threw up the window.

"It's not for sale, for gold or money," said the lassie.

"If it's not for sale for gold or money, what is it that you will sell it for? You may name your own price," said the Princess.

"Well! if I may get to the Prince, who lives here, and be with him to-night, you shall have it," said the lassie whom the North Wind had brought.

Yes! she might; that could be done. So the Princess got the gold apple; but when the lassie came up to the Prince's bed-room at night he was fast asleep; she called him and shook him, and between whiles she wept sore; but all she could do she couldn't wake him up. Next morning as soon as day broke, came the Princess with the long nose, and drove her out again.

So in the day-time she sat down under the castle windows

and began to card with her golden carding-comb, and the same thing happened. The Princess asked what she wanted for it; and she said it wasn't for sale for gold or money, but if she might get leave to go up to the Prince and be with him that night, the Princess should have it. But when she went up she found him fast asleep again, and all she called, and all she shook, and wept, and prayed, she couldn't get life into him; and as soon as the first gray peep of day came, then came the Princess with the long nose, and chased her out again.

So in the day-time the lassie sat down outside under the castle window, and began to spin with her golden spinning-wheel, and that, too, the Princess with the long nose wanted to have. So she threw up the window and asked what she wanted for it. The lassie said, as she had said twice before, it wasn't for sale for gold or money; but if she might go up to the Prince who was there, and be with him alone that night, she might have it.

Yes! she might do that and welcome. But now you must know there were some Christian folk who had been carried off thither, and as they sat in their room, which was next the Prince, they had heard how a woman had been in there, and wept and prayed, and called to him two nights running, and they told that to the Prince.

That evening, when the Princess came with her sleepy drink, the Prince made as if he drank, but threw it over his shoulder, for he could guess it was a sleepy drink. So, when the lassie came in, she found the Prince wide awake; and then she told him the whole story how she had come thither.

"Ah," said the Prince, "you've just come in the very nick of time, for to-morrow is to be our wedding-day; but now I won't have the Long-nose, and you are the only woman in the world who can set me free. I'll say I want to see what my wife is fit for, and beg her to wash the shirt which has the three spots of wax on it; she'll say yes, for she doesn't know 'tis you who put them there; but that's a work only for Christian folk, and not for such a pack of Trolls, and so I'll say that I won't have any other for my bride than the woman who can wash them out, and ask you to do it."

So there was great joy and love between them all that night. But next day, when the wedding was to be, the Prince said—

"First of all, I'd like to see what my bride is fit for."

"Yes!" said the stepmother, with all her heart.

"Well," said the Prince, "I've got a fine shirt which I'd like for my wedding shirt, but some how or other it has got three spots of wax on it, which I must have washed out; and I have sworn never to take any other bride than the woman who's able to do that. If she can't, she's not worth having."

Well, that was no great thing they said, so they agreed, and she with the long nose began to wash away as hard as she could, but the more she rubbed and scrubbed, the bigger the spots grew.

"Ah," said the old hag, her mother, "you can't wash; let me try."

But she hadn't long taken the shirt in her hand, before it got far worse than ever, and with all her rubbing, and wringing, and scrubbing, the spots grew bigger and blacker, and the darker and uglier was the shirt.

Then all the other Trolls began to wash, but the longer it lasted, the blacker and uglier the shirt grew, till at last it was as black all over as if it had been up the chimney.

"Ah!" said the Prince, "you're none of you worth a straw: you can't wash. Why there, outside, sits a beggar lassie, I'll be bound she knows how to wash better than the whole lot of you. COME IN, LASSIE!" he shouted.

Well, in she came.

"Can you wash this shirt clean, lassie, you?" said he.

"I don't know," she said, "but I think I can."

And almost before she had taken it and dipped it in the water, it was as white as driven snow, and whiter still.

"Yes; you are the lassie for me," said the Prince.

At that the old hag flew into such a rage, she burst on the spot, and the Princess with the long nose after her, and the whole pack of Trolls after her—at least I've never heard a word about them since.

As for the Prince and Princess, they set free all the poor Christian folk who had been carried off and shut up there; and they took with them all the silver and gold, and flitted away as far as they could from the castle that lay EAST O' THE SUN AND WEST O' THE MOON.

Why the Sea Is Salt

ONCE ON a time, but it was a long, long time ago, there were two brothers, one rich and one poor. Now, one Christmas eve, the poor one hadn't so much as a crumb in the house, either of meat or bread, so he went to his brother to ask him for something to keep Christmas with, in God's name. It was not the first time his brother had been forced to help him, and you may fancy he wasn't very glad to see his face, but he said—

"If you will do what I ask you to do, I'll give you a whole side of bacon."

So the poor brother said he would do anything, and was full of thanks.

"Well, here is the bacon," said the rich brother, "and now go straight to Hell."

"What I have given my word to do, I must stick to," said the other; so he took the side of bacon and set off. He walked the whole day, and at dusk he came to a place where he saw a very bright light.

"Maybe this is the place," said the man to himself. So he turned aside, and the first thing he saw was an old, old man, with a long white beard, who stood in a shed, chopping wood for the Christmas fire.

"Good even," said the man with the bacon.

"The same to you; whither are you going so late?" said the man.

"Oh! I'm going to Hell, if I only knew the right way," answered the poor man.

"Well, you're not far wrong, for this is Hell," said the old man; "when you get inside they will be all for buying your bacon, for meat is scarce in Hell; but mind you don't sell

13

it unless you get the hand-quern which stands behind the door for it. When you come out, I'll teach you how to handle the quern, for it's good to grind almost anything."

So the man with the bacon thanked the other for his good advice, and gave a great knock at the Devil's door.

When he got in, everything went just as the old man had said. All the devils, great and small, came swarming up to him like ants round an anthill, and each tried to out-bid the other for the bacon.

"Well!" said the man, "by rights my old dame and I ought to have this bacon for our Christmas dinner; but since you have all set your hearts on it, I suppose I must give it up to you; but if I sell it at all, I'll have for it that quern behind the door yonder."

At first the Devil wouldn't hear of such a bargain, and bartered and haggled with the man; but he stuck to what he said, and at last the Devil had to part with his quern. When the man got out into the yard, he asked the old woodcutter how he was to handle the quern; and after he had learned how to use it, he thanked the old man and went off home as fast as he could, but still the clock had struck twelve on Christmas eve before he reached his own door.

"Wherever in the world have you been?" said his old dame; "here have I sat hour after hour waiting and watching, without so much as two sticks to lay together under the Christmas dinner."

"Oh!" said the man, "I couldn't get back before, for I had to go a long way first for one thing, and then for another; but now you shall see what you shall see."

So he put the quern on the table, and bade it first of all grind lights, then a table-cloth, then meat, then ale, and so on till they had got everything that was nice for Christmas fare. He had only to speak the word, and the quern ground out what he wanted. The old dame stood by blessing her stars, and kept on asking where he had got this wonderful quern, but he wouldn't tell her.

"It's all one where I got it from; you see the quern is a

good one, and the mill-stream never freezes, that's enough."

So he ground meat and drink and dainties enough to last out till Twelfth Day, and on the third day he asked all his friends and kin to his house, and gave a great feast. Now, when his rich brother saw all that was on the table, and all that was behind in the larder, he grew quite spiteful and wild, for he couldn't bear that his brother should have anything.

"'Twas only on Christmas eve," he said to the rest, "he was in such straits that he came and asked for a morsel of food in God's name, and now he gives a feast as if he were count or king"; and he turned to his brother and said—

"But whence, in Hell's name, have you got all this wealth?"

"From behind the door," answered the owner of the quern, for he didn't care to let the cat out of the bag. But later on the evening, when he had got a drop too much, he could keep his secret no longer, and brought out the quern and said—

"There, you see what has gotten me all this wealth"; and so he made the quern grind all kind of things. When his brother saw it, he set his heart on having the quern, and, after a deal of coaxing, he got it; but he had to pay three hundred dollars for it, and his brother bargained to keep it till hay-harvest, for he thought, if I keep it till then, I can make it grind meat and drink that will last for years. So you may fancy the quern didn't grow rusty for want of work, and when hay-harvest came, the rich brother got it, but the other took care not to teach him how to handle it.

It was evening when the rich brother got the quern home, and next morning he told his wife to go out into the hay-field and toss, while the mowers cut the grass, and he would stay at home and get the dinner ready. So, when dinner-time drew near, he put the quern on the kitchen table and said—

"Grind herrings and broth, and grind them good and fast."

So the quern began to grind herrings and broth; first of all, all the dishes full, then all the tubs full, and so on till the kitchen floor was quite covered. Then the man twisted and twirled at the quern to get it to stop, but for all his twisting and fingering the quern went on grinding, and in a little while the broth rose so high that the man was like to drown. So he threw open the kitchen door and ran into the parlour, but it wasn't long before the quern had ground the parlour full too, and it was only at the risk of his life that the man could get hold of the latch of the house door through the stream of broth. When he got the door open, he ran out and set off down the road, with the stream of herrings and broth at his heels, roaring like a waterfall over the whole farm.

Now, his old dame, who was in the field tossing hay, thought it a long time to dinner, and at last she said—

"Well! though the master doesn't call us home, we may as well go. Maybe he finds it hard to boil the broth, and will be glad of my help."

The men were willing enough, so they sauntered homewards; but just as they had got a little way up the hill, what should they meet but herrings, and broth, and bread, all running and dashing, and splashing together in a stream, and the master himself running before them for his life, and as he passed them he bawled out—"Would to heaven each of you had a hundred throats! but take care you're not drowned in the broth."

Away he went, as though the Evil One were at his heels, to his brother's house, and begged him for God's sake to take back the quern that instant; for, said he—

"If it grinds only one hour more, the whole parish will be swallowed up by herrings and broth."

But his brother wouldn't hear of taking it back till the other paid him down three hundred dollars more.

So the poor brother got both the money and the quern, and it wasn't long before he set up a farm-house far finer than the one in which his brother lived, and with the quern he ground so much gold that he covered it with plates of gold; and as the farm lay by the sea-side, the golden house gleamed and glistened far away over the sea. All who sailed by put ashore to see the rich man in the golden house, and to see the wonderful quern, the fame of which spread far and wide, till there was nobody who hadn't heard tell of it.

So one day there came a skipper who wanted to see the quern; and the first thing he asked was if it could grind salt.

"Grind salt!" said the owner; "I should just think it could. It can grind anything."

When the skipper heard that, he said he must have the quern, cost what it would; for if he only had it, he thought he should be rid of his long voyages across stormy seas for a lading of salt. Well, at first the man wouldn't hear of parting with the quern; but the skipper begged and prayed so hard, that at last he let him have it, but he had to pay many, many thousand dollars for it. Now, when the skipper had got the quern on his back, he soon made off with it, for he was afraid lest the man should change his mind; so he had no time to ask how to handle the quern, but got on board his ship as fast as he could, and set sail. When he had sailed a good way off, he brought the quern on deck and said—

"Grind salt, and grind both good and fast."

Well, the quern began to grind salt so that it poured out like water; and when the skipper had got the ship full, he wished to stop the quern, but whichever way he turned it, and however much he tried, it was no good; the quern kept grinding on, and the heap of salt grew higher and higher, and at last down sunk the ship.

There lies the quern at the bottom of the sea, and grinds away at this very day, and that's why the sea is salt.

The Twelve Wild Ducks

ONCE ON a time there was a Queen who was out driving, when there had been a new fall of snow in the winter; but when she had gone a little way, she began to bleed at the nose, and had to get out of her sledge. And so, as she stood there, leaning against the fence, and saw the red blood on the white snow, she fell a-thinking how she had twelve sons and no daughter, and she said to herself—

"If I only had a daughter as white as snow and as red as blood, I shouldn't care what became of all my sons."

But the words were scarce out of her mouth before an old witch of the Trolls came up to her.

"A daughter you shall have," she said, "and she shall be as white as snow, and as red as blood; and your sons shall be mine, but you may keep them till the babe is christened."

So when the time came the Queen had a daughter, and she was as white as snow, and as red as blood, just as the Troll had promised, and so they called her "Snow-white and Rosy-red." Well, there was great joy at the King's court, and the Queen was as glad as glad could be; but when what she had promised to the old witch came into her mind, she sent for a silversmith, and bade him make twelve silver spoons, one for each prince, and after that she bade him make one more, and that she gave to Snow-white and Rosy-red. But as soon as ever the Princess was christened, the Princes were turned into twelve wild ducks, and flew away. They never saw them again,—away they went, and away they stayed.

So the Princess grew up, and she was both tall and fair, but she was often so strange and sorrowful, and no one

18

could understand what it was that failed her. But one evening the Queen was also sorrowful, for she had many strange thoughts when she thought of her sons. She said to Snow-white and Rosy-red—

"Why are you so sorrowful, my daughter? Is there anything you want? if so, only say the word, and you shall have it."

"Oh, it seems so dull and lonely here," said Snow-white and Rosy-red; "every one else has brothers and sisters, but I am all alone; I have none; and that's why I'm so sorrowful."

"But you *had* brothers, my daughter," said the Queen; "I had twelve sons who were your brothers, but I gave them all away to get you"; and so she told her the whole story.

So when the Princess heard that, she had no rest; for, in spite of all the Queen could say or do, and all she wept and prayed, the lassie would set off to seek her brothers, for she thought it was all her fault; and at last she got leave to go away from the palace. On and on she walked into the wide world, so far, you would never have thought a young lady could have strength to walk so far.

So, once, when she was walking through a great, great wood, one day she felt tired, and sat down on a mossy tuft and fell asleep. Then she dreamt that she went deeper and deeper into the wood, till she came to a little wooden hut, and there she found her brothers; just then she woke, and straight before her she saw a worn path in the green moss, and this path went deeper into the wood; so she followed it, and after a long time she came to just such a little wooden house as that she had seen in her dream.

Now, when she went into the room there was no one at home, but there stood twelve beds, and twelve chairs, and twelve spoons—a dozen of everything, in short. So when she saw that she was so glad, she hadn't been so glad for many a long year, for she could guess at once that her brothers lived here, and that they owned the beds, and chairs, and spoons. So she began to make up the fire, and sweep the room, and make the beds, and cook the dinner, and to make the house as tidy as she could; and when she had done all the cooking and work, she ate her own dinner, and crept under her youngest brother's bed, and lay down there, but she forgot her spoon upon the table.

So she had scarcely laid herself down before she heard something flapping and whirring in the air, and so all the twelve wild ducks came sweeping in; but as soon as ever they crossed the threshold they became Princes.

"Oh, how nice and warm it is in here," they said. "Heaven bless him who made up the fire, and cooked such a good dinner for us."

And so each took up his silver spoon and was going to eat. But when each had taken his own, there was one still left lying on the table, and it was so like the rest that they couldn't tell it from them.

"This is our sister's spoon," they said; "and if her spoon be here, she can't be very far off herself."

"If this be our sister's spoon, and she be here," said the eldest, "she shall be killed, for she is to blame for all the ill we suffer."

And this she lay under the bed and listened to.

"No," said the youngest, "'twere a shame to kill her for that. She has nothing to do with our suffering ill; for if any one's to blame, it's our own mother."

So they set to work hunting for her both high and low, and at last they looked under all the beds, and so when they came to the youngest Prince's bed, they found her, and dragged her out. Then the eldest Prince wished again to have her killed, but she begged and prayed so prettily for herself.

"Oh! gracious goodness! don't kill me, for I've gone about seeking you these three years, and if I could only set you free, I'd willingly lose my life."

"Well!" said they, "if you will set us free, you may keep your life; for you can if you choose."

"Yes; only tell me," said the Princess, "how it can be done, and I'll do it, whatever it be."

"You must pick thistle-down," said the Princes, "and you must card it, and spin it, and weave it; and after you have done that, you must cut out and make twelve coats, and twelve shirts, and twelve neckerchiefs, one for each of us, and while you do that, you must neither talk, nor laugh, nor weep. If you can do that, we are free."

"But where shall I ever get thistle-down enough for so many neckerchiefs, and shirts, and coats?" asked Snow-white and Rosy-red.

"We'll show you," said the Princes; and so they took her with them to a great wide moor, where there stood such a crop of thistles, all nodding and nodding in the breeze, and the down all floating and glistening like spiderwebs through the air in the sunbeams. The Princess had never seen such a quantity of thistle-down in her life, and she began to pluck and gather it as fast and as well as she could; and when she got home at night she set to work carding and spinning yarn from the down. So she went on a long long time, picking, and carding, and spinning, and all the while keeping the Princes' house, cooking, and making their beds. At evening home they came, flapping and whirring like wild ducks, and all night they were Princes, but in the morning off they flew again, and were wild ducks the whole day.

But now it happened once, when she was out on the moor to pick thistle-down,—and if I don't mistake, it was the very last time she was to go thither,—it happened that the young King who ruled that land was out hunting, and came riding across the moor, and saw her. So he stopped there and wondered who the lovely lady could be that walked along the moor picking thistle-down, and he asked her her name, and when he could get no answer, he was still more astonished; and at last he liked her so much, that nothing would do but he must take her home to his castle and marry her. So he ordered his servants to take her and put her up on his horse. Snow-white and Rosy-red she wrung her hands, and made signs to them, and pointed to the bags in which her work was, and when the

King saw she wished to have them with her, he told his men to take up the bags behind them. When they had done that the Princess came to herself, little by little, for the King was both a wise man and a handsome man too, and he was as soft and kind to her as a doctor. But when they got home to the palace, and the old Queen, who was his stepmother, set eyes on Snow-white and Rosy-red, she got so cross and jealous of her because she was so lovely, that she said to the king—

"Can't you see now, that this thing whom you have picked up, and whom you are going to marry, is a witch? Why, she can't either talk, or laugh, or weep!"

But the King didn't care a pin for what she said, but held on with the wedding, and married Snow-white and Rosy-red, and they lived in great joy and glory; but she didn't forget to go on sewing at her shirts.

So when the year was almost out, Snow-white and Rosy-red brought a Prince into the world; and then the old Queen was more spiteful and jealous than ever, and at dead of night she stole in to Snow-white and Rosy-red, while she slept, and took away her babe, and threw it into a pit full of snakes. After that she cut Snow-white and Rosy-red in her finger, and smeared the blood over her mouth, and went straight to the King.

"Now come and see," she said, "what sort of a thing you have taken for your Queen; here she has eaten up her own babe."

Then the king was so downcast, he almost burst into tears, and said—

"Yes, it must be true, since I see it with my own eyes; but she'll not do it again, I'm sure, and so this time I'll spare her life."

So before the next year was out she had another son, and the same thing happened. The King's stepmother got more and more jealous and spiteful. She stole into the young Queen at night while she slept, took away the babe, and threw it into a pit full of snakes, cut the young Queen's finger, and smeared the blood over her mouth, and then went and told the King she had eaten up her own child. Then the King was so sorrowful, you can't think how sorry he was, and he said—

"Yes, it must be true, since I see it with my own eyes, but she'll not do it again, I'm sure, and so this time too I'll spare her life."

Well, before the next year was out, Snow-white and Rosy-red brought a daughter into the world, and her, too, the old Queen took and threw into the pit full of snakes, while the young Queen slept. Then she cut her finger, smeared the blood over her mouth, and went again to the King and said—

"Now you may come and see if it isn't as I say; she's a wicked, wicked witch, for here she has gone and eaten up her third babe too."

Then the King was so sad, there was no end to it, for now he couldn't spare her any longer, but had to order her to be burnt alive on a pile of wood. But just when the pile was all ablaze, and they were going to put her on it, she made signs to them to take twelve boards and lay them round the pile, and on these she laid the neckerchiefs, and the shirts, and the coats for her brothers, but the youngest brother's shirt wanted its left arm, for she hadn't had time to finish it. And as soon as ever she had done that, they heard such a flapping and whirring in the air, and down came twelve wild ducks flying over the forest, and each of them snapped up his clothes in his bill and flew off with them.

"See now!" said the old Queen to the King, "wasn't I right when I told you she was a witch; but make haste and burn her before the pile burns low."

"Oh!" said the King, "we've wood enough and to spare, and so I'll wait a bit, for I have a mind to see what the end of all this will be."

As he spoke, up came the twelve princes riding along, as handsome well-grown lads as you'd wish to see; but the youngest prince had a wild duck's wing instead of his left arm.

"What's all this about?" asked the Princes.

"My Queen is to be burnt," said the King, "because she's a witch, and because she has eaten up her own babes."

"She hasn't eaten them at all," said the Princes. "Speak now, sister; you have set us free and saved us, now save yourself."

Then Snow-white and Rosy-red spoke, and told the whole story; how every time she was brought to bed, the old Queen, the King's stepmother, had stolen into her at night, had taken her babes away, and cut her little finger, and smeared the blood over her mouth; and then the Princes took the King, and showed him the snake-pit where three babes lay playing with adders and toads, and lovelier children you never saw.

So the King had them taken out at once, and went to his stepmother, and asked her what punishment she thought that woman deserved who could find it in her heart to betray a guiltless Queen and three such blessed little babes.

"She deserves to be fast bound between twelve unbroken steeds, so that each may take his share of her," said the old Queen.

"You have spoken your own doom," said the King, "and you shall suffer it at once."

So the wicked old Queen was fast bound between twelve unbroken steeds, and each got his share of her. But the King took Snow-white and Rosy-red, and their three children, and the twelve Princes; and so they all went home to their father and mother, and told all that had befallen them, and there was joy and gladness over the whole kingdom, because the Princess was saved and set free, and because she had set free her twelve brothers.

The Mastermaid

ONCE ON a time there was a king who had several sons—I don't know how many there were—but the youngest had no rest at home, for nothing else would please him but to go out into the world and try his luck, and after a long time the king was forced to give him leave to go. Now, after he had travelled some days, he came one night to a Giant's house, and there he got a place in the Giant's service. In the morning the Giant went off to herd his goats, and as he left the yard he told the Prince to clean out the stable; "And after you have done that, you needn't do anything else to-day; for you must know it is an easy master you have come to. But what is set you to do you must do well, and you mustn't think of going into any of the rooms which are beyond that in which you slept, for if you do, I'll take your life."

"Sure enough, it is an easy master I have got," said the Prince to himself, as he walked up and down the room, and danced and sang, for he thought there was plenty of time to clean out the stable.

"But still it would be good fun just to peep into his other rooms, for there must be something in them which he is afraid lest I should see, since he won't give me leave to go in."

So he went into the first room, and there was a pot boiling on a hook by the wall, but the Prince saw no fire underneath it. I wonder what is inside it, he thought; and then he dipped a lock of his hair into it, and the hair seemed as if it were all turned to copper.

"What a dainty broth," he said; "if one tasted it, he'd look grand inside his gut"; and with that he went into the next room. There, too, was a pot hanging by a hook, which

25

bubbled and boiled; but there was no fire under that either.

"I may as well try this too," said the Prince, as he put another lock into the pot, and it came out all silvered.

"They haven't such rich broth in my father's house," said the Prince; "but it all depends on how it tastes," and with that he went on into the third room. There, too, hung a pot, and boiled just as he had seen in the two other rooms, and the Prince had a mind to try this too, so he dipped a lock of hair into it, and it came out golden, so that the light gleamed from it.

"'Worse and worse,' said the old wife; but I say better and better," said the Prince; "but if he boils gold here, I wonder what he boils in yonder."

He thought he might as well see; so he went through the door into the fourth room. Well, there was no pot in there, but there was a Princess, seated on a bench, so lovely, that the Prince had never seen anything like her in his born days.

"Oh! in Heaven's name," she said, "what do you want here?"

"I got a place here yesterday," said the Prince.

"A place, indeed! Heaven help you out of it."

"Well, after all, I think I've got an easy master; he hasn't set me much to do to-day, for after I have cleaned out the stable my day's work is over."

"Yes, but how will you do it?" she said; "for if you set to work to clean it like other folk, ten pitchforks full will come in for every one you toss out. But I will teach you how to set to work; you must turn the fork upside down, and toss with the handle, and then all the dung will fly out of itself."

"Yes, he would be sure to do that," said the Prince; and so he sat there the whole day, for he and the Princess were soon great friends, and had made up their minds to have one another, and so the first day of his service with the Giant was not long, you may fancy. But when the evening drew on, she said 'twould be as well if he got the stable cleaned out before the Giant came home; and when he went to the stable he thought he would just see if what she had said were true, and so he began to work like the grooms in his father's stable; but he soon had enough of that, for he hadn't worked a minute before the stable was so full of dung that he hadn't room to stand. Then he did as the Princess bade him, and turned up the fork and worked with the handle, and lo! in a flash the stable was as clean as if it had been scoured. And when he had done his work he went back into the room where the Giant had given him leave to be, and began to walk up and down, and to dance and sing. So after a bit, home came the Giant with his goats.

"Have you cleaned the stable?" asked the Giant.

"Yes, now it's all right and tight, master," answered the Prince.

"I'll soon see if it is," growled the Giant, and strode off to the stable, where he found it just as the Prince had said.

"You've been talking to my Mastermaid, I can see," said the Giant; "for you've not come upon this knowledge on your own."

"Mastermaid!" said the Prince, who looked as stupid as an owl, "what sort of thing is that, master? I'd be very glad to see it."

"Well, well!" said the Giant; "you'll see her soon enough."

Next day the Giant set off with his goats again, and before he went he told the Prince to fetch home his horse, which was out grazing on the hill-side, and when he had done that he might rest all the day.

"For you must know it is an easy master you have come to," said the Giant; "but if you go into any of the rooms I spoke of yesterday, I'll wring your head off."

So off he went with his flock of goats.

"An easy master you are indeed," said the Prince; "but for all that, I'll just go in and have a chat with your Master-maid; may be she'll be as soon mine as yours." So he went in to her, and she asked him what he had to do that day.

"Oh! nothing to be afraid of," said he; "I've only to go up to the hill-side to fetch his horse."

"Very well; and how will you set about it?"

"Well, for that matter, there's no great art in riding a horse home. I fancy I've ridden fresher horses before now," said the Prince.

"Ah, but this isn't so easy a task as you think; but I'll teach you how to do it. When you get near it, fire and flame will come out of its nostrils, as out of a tar barrel; but look out, and take the bit which hangs behind the door yonder, and throw it right into his jaws, and he will grow so tame that you may do what you like with him."

Yes! the Prince would mind and do that; and so he sat in there the whole day, talking and chattering with the Mastermaid about one thing and another; but they always came back to how happy they would be if they could only have one another, and get well away from the Giant; and, to tell the truth, the Prince would have clean forgotten both the horse and the hill-side, if the Mastermaid hadn't put him in mind of them when evening drew on, telling him he had better set out to fetch the horse before the Giant came home. So he set off, and took the bit which hung in the corner, ran up the hill, and it wasn't long before he met the horse, with fire and flame streaming out of its nostrils. But he watched his time, and as the horse came open-jawed up to him, he threw the bit into its mouth, and it stood as quiet as a lamb. After that it was no great matter to ride it home and put it up, you may fancy; and then the Prince went into his room again, and began to dance and sing.

So the Giant came home again at evening with his goats; and the first words he said were—

"Have you brought my horse down from the hill?"

"Yes, master, that I have," said the Prince; "and a better horse I never rode; but for all that I rode him straight home, and put him up safe and sound."

"I'll soon see to that," said the Giant, and ran out to

the stable, and there stood the horse just as the Prince had said.

"You've talked to my Mastermaid, I'll be bound, for you haven't come upon this knowledge on your own," said the Giant again.

"Yesterday master talked of this Mastermaid, and to-day it's the same story," said the Prince, who pretended to be silly and stupid. "Bless you, master! why don't you show me the thing at once? I should so like to see it only once in my life."

"Oh, if that's all," said the Giant, "you'll see her soon enough."

The third day, at dawn, the Giant went off to the wood again with his goats; but before he went he said to the Prince—

"To-day you must go to Hell and fetch my fire-tax. When you have done that you can rest yourself all day, for you must know it is an easy master you have come to," and with that off he went.

"Easy master, indeed!" said the Prince. "You may be easy, but you set me hard tasks all the same. But I may as well see if I can find your Mastermaid, as you call her. I daresay she'll tell me what to do," and so in he went to her again.

So when the Mastermaid asked what the Giant had set him to do that day, he told her how he was to go to Hell and fetch the fire-tax.

"And how will you set about it?" asked the Mastermaid.

"Oh, that you must tell me," said the Prince. "I have never been to Hell in my life; and even if I knew the way, I don't know how much I am to ask for."

"Well, I'll soon tell you," said the Mastermaid; "you must go to the steep rock away yonder, under the hill-side, and take the club that lies there, and knock on the face of the rock. Then there will come out one all glistening with fire; to him you must tell your errand; and when he asks you how much you will have, mind you say, 'As much as I can carry.'"

Yes; he would be sure to say that; so he sat in there with
the Mastermaid all that day too; and though evening drew
on, he would have sat there till now, had not the Mastermaid put him in mind it was high time to be off to Hell to
fetch the Giant's fire-tax before he came home. So he went
on his way, and did just as the Mastermaid had told him;
and when he reached the rock he took up the club and
gave a great thump. Then the rock opened, and out came
one whose face glistened, and out of whose eyes and nostrils flew sparks of fire.

"What is your will?" said he.

"Oh! I'm only come from the Giant to fetch his fire-tax,"
said the Prince.

"How much will you have then?" said the other.

"I never wish for more than I am able to carry," said
the Prince.

"Lucky for you that you did not ask for a whole horse-
load," said he who came out of the rock; "but come now
into the rock with me, and you shall have it."

So the Prince went in with him, and you may fancy what
heaps and heaps of gold and silver he saw lying in there,
just like stones in a gravel-pit; and he got a load just as big
as he was able to carry, and set off home with it. Now,
when the Giant came home with his goats at evening, the
Prince went into his room, and began to dance and sing as
he had done the evenings before.

"Have you been to Hell after my fire-tax?" roared the
Giant.

"Oh yes; that I have, master," answered the Prince.

"Where have you put it?" said the Giant.

"There stands the sack on the bench yonder," said
the Prince.

"I'll soon see to that," said the Giant, who strode off to
the bench, and there he saw the sack so full that the gold
and silver dropped out on the floor as soon as ever he
untied the string.

"You've been talking to my Mastermaid, that I can see,"
said the Giant; "but if you have, I'll wring your head off."

"Mastermaid!" said the Prince; "yesterday master talked of this Mastermaid, and to-day he talks of her again, and the day before yesterday it was the same story. I only wish I could see what sort of thing she is! that I do."

"Well, well, wait till to-morrow," said the Giant, "and then I'll take you in to her myself."

"Thank you kindly, master," said the Prince; "but it's only a joke of master's, I'll be bound."

So next day the Giant took him in to the Mastermaid, and said to her—

"Now, you must cut his throat, and boil him in the great big pot—you know the one; and when the broth is ready just give me a call."

After that he laid him down on the bench to sleep, and began to snore so, that it sounded like thunder on the hills.

So the Mastermaid took a knife and cut the Prince in his little finger, and let three drops of blood fall on a three-legged stool; and after that she took all the old rags and soles of shoes, and all the rubbish she could lay hands on, and put them into the pot; and then she filled a chest full of ground gold, and took a lump of salt, and a flask of water that hung behind the door, and she took, besides, a golden apple, and two golden chickens, and off she set with the Prince from the Giant's house as fast as they could; and when they had gone a little way, they came to the sea, and after that they sailed over the sea; but where they got the ship from I have never heard tell.

So when the Giant had slumbered a good bit, he began to stretch himself as he lay on the bench, and called out, "Will it be soon done?"

"Only just begun," answered the first drop of blood on the stool.

So the Giant lay down to sleep again, and slumbered a long, long time. At last he began to toss about a little, and cried out—

"Do you hear what I say; will it be soon done?" but he

did not look up this time any more than the first, for he was still half asleep.

"Half done," said the second drop of blood.

Then the Giant thought again it was the Mastermaid, so he turned over on his other side, and fell asleep again; and when he had gone on sleeping for many hours, he began to stir and stretch his old bones, and to call out—

"Isn't it done yet?"

"Done to a turn," said the third drop of blood.

Then the Giant rose up, and began to rub his eyes, but he couldn't see who it was that was talking to him, so he searched and called for the Mastermaid, but no one answered.

"Ah, well! I dare say she's just run out of doors for a bit," he thought, and took up a spoon and went up to the pot to taste the broth; but he found nothing but shoesoles, and rags, and such stuff; and it was all boiled up together, so that he couldn't tell which was thick and which was thin. As soon as he saw this, he could tell how things had gone, and he got so angry he scarce knew which leg to stand upon. Away he went after the Prince and the Mastermaid, till the wind whistled behind him; but before long he came to the water and couldn't cross it.

"Never mind," he said; "I know a cure for this. I've only got to call on my stream-sucker."

So he called on his stream-sucker, and he came and stooped down, and took one, two, three, gulps; and then the water fell so much in the sea that the Giant could see the Mastermaid and the Prince sailing in their ship.

"Now you must cast out the lump of salt," said the Mastermaid.

So the Prince threw it overboard, and it grew up into a mountain so high, right across the sea, that the Giant couldn't pass it, and the stream-sucker couldn't help him by swilling any more water.

"Never mind," cried the Giant; "there's a cure for this too. So he called on his hill-borer to come and bore through the mountain, that the stream-sucker might creep through and take another swill; but just as they had made a hole through the hill, and the stream-sucker was about to drink, the Mastermaid told the Prince to throw overboard a drop or two out of the flask, and then the sea was just as full as ever, and before the stream-sucker could take another gulp, they reached the land and were saved from the Giant.

So they made up their minds to go home to the Prince's father; but the Prince would not hear of the Mastermaid's walking, for he thought it seemly neither for her nor for him.

"Just wait here ten minutes," he said, "while I go home after the seven horses which stand in my father's stall. It's no great way off, and I shan't be long about it; but I will not hear of my sweetheart walking to my father's palace."

"Ah!" said the Mastermaid, "pray don't leave me, for if you once get home to the palace you'll forget me outright; I know you will."

"Oh!" said he, "how can I forget you; you with whom I have gone through so much, and whom I love so dearly?"

There was no help for it, he must and would go home to fetch the coach and seven horses, and she was to wait for him by the sea-side. So at last the Mastermaid was forced to let him have his way; she only said—

"Now, when you get home, don't stop so much as to say good day to any one, but go straight to the stable and put to the horses, and drive back as quick as you can; for they will all come about you, but do as though you did not see them; and above all things, mind you do not taste a morsel of food, for if you do, we shall both come to grief."

All this the Prince promised; but he thought all the time there was little fear of his forgetting her.

Now, just as he came home to the palace, one of his brothers was thinking of holding his bridal feast, and the bride, and all her kith and kin, were just come to the palace. So they all gathered round him, and asked about this thing and that, and wanted him to go in with them; but he made as though he did not see them, and went straight to the stall and got out the horses, and began to put them to. And when they saw they could not get him to go in, they came out to him with meat and drink, and the best of everything they had got ready for the feast; but the Prince would not taste so much as a crumb, and worked as fast as he could. At last the bride's sister rolled an apple across the yard to him, saying—

"Well, if you won't eat anything else, you may as well take a bite of this, for you must be both hungry and thirsty after so long a journey."

So he took up the apple and bit a piece out of it; but he had scarce done so before he forgot the Mastermaid, and how he was to drive back for her.

"Well, I think I must be mad," he said; "what am I to do with this coach and horses?"

So he put the horses up again, and went along with the others into the palace, and it was soon settled that he should have the bride's sister, who had rolled the apple over to him.

There sat the Mastermaid by the sea-shore, and waited and waited for the Prince, but no Prince came; so at last she went up from the shore, and after she had gone a bit she came to a little hut, which lay by itself in a grove close by the king's palace. She went in and asked if she might lodge there. It was an old dame that owned the hut, and a stubborn scolding hag she was as ever you saw. At first she would not hear of the Mastermaid's lodging in her house, but at last, for fair words and high rent, the Mastermaid got leave to be there. Now the hut was as dark and dirty as a pigsty, so the Mastermaid said she would smarten it up a little, that their house might look inside like other people's. The old hag did not like this either, and showed her teeth, and was cross; but the Mastermaid did not mind her. She took her chest of gold, and threw a handful or so into the fire, and lo! the gold melted, and bubbled and boiled over out of the grate, and spread itself over the whole hut, till it was gilded both outside and in. But as soon as the gold began to bubble and boil, the old hag got so afraid that she tried to run out as if the Evil One were at her heels; and as she ran out at the door, she forgot to stoop, and gave her head such a knock against the door-frame, that she broke her neck, and that was the end of her.

Next morning the Constable passed that way, and you may fancy he could scarce believe his eyes when he saw the golden hut shining and glistening away in the grove; but he was still more astonished when he went in and saw the lovely maiden who sat there. To make a long story short, he fell over head and ears in love with her, and begged and prayed her to become his wife.

"Well, but have you much money?" asked the Mastermaid.

Yes, for that matter, he said, he was not so badly off, and off he went home to fetch the money, and when he came back at even he brought a half-bushel sack, and set it down on the bench. So the Mastermaid said she would have him, since he was so rich; but they were scarce in bed before she said she must get up again—

"For I have forgotten to make up the fire."

"Pray, don't stir out of bed," said the Constable; "I'll see to it."

So he jumped out of bed, and stood on the hearth in a flash.

"As soon as you have got hold of the shovel, just tell me," said the Mastermaid.

"Well, I am holding it now," said the Constable.

Then the Mastermaid said—

"God grant that you may hold the shovel, and the shovel you, and may you heap hot burning coals over yourself till morning breaks."

So there stood the Constable all night long, shovelling hot burning coals over himself; and though he begged, and prayed, and wept, the coals were not a bit colder for that; but as soon as day broke, and he had power to cast away the shovel, he did not stay long, as you may fancy, but set off as if the Evil One or the bailiff were at his heels;

and all who met him stared their eyes out at him, for he
cut capers as though he were mad, and he could not have
looked in worse plight if he had been skinned and tanned,
and every one wondered what had befallen him, but he
told no one where he had been, for shame's sake.

Next day the Attorney passed by the place where the
Mastermaid lived, and he too saw it shone and glistened
in the grove; so he turned aside to find out who owned the
hut; and when he came in and saw the lovely maiden, he
fell more in love with her than the Constable, and began
to woo her in hot haste.

Well, the Mastermaid asked him, as she had asked the
Constable, if he had a good lot of money? and the Attorney said he wasn't so badly off; and as a proof he went
home to fetch his money. So at even he came back with a
great fat sack of money—I think it was a whole bushel
sack—and set it down on the bench; and the long and the
short of the matter was, that he was to have her, and they
went to bed. But all at once the Mastermaid had forgotten
to shut the door of the porch, and she must get up and
make it fast for the night.

"What, you do that!" said the Attorney, "while I lie here;
that can never be; lie still while I go and do it."

So up he jumped like a pea on a drum-head, and ran out
into the porch.

"Tell me," said the Mastermaid, "when you have hold of
the door-latch."

"I've got hold of it now," said the Attorney.

"God grant, then," said the Mastermaid, "that you may
hold the door, and the door you, and that you may go
from wall to wall till day dawns."

So you may fancy what a dance the Attorney had all
night long; such a waltz he never had before, and I don't
think he would much care if he never had such a waltz
again. Now he pulled the door forward, and then the door
pulled him back, and so he went on, now dashed into one
corner of the porch, and now into the other, till he was
almost battered to death. At first he began to curse and

Well! they sent another message to the grove, and asked so prettily if they couldn't have the loan of the golden porch-door which the Attorney had talked of; and they got it on the spot. So they were just setting out; but now the horses were not strong enough to draw the coach, though there were six of them; then they put on eight, and ten, and twelve, but the more they put on, and the more the coachman whipped, the more the coach wouldn't stir an inch. By this time it was far on in the day, and every one about the palace was in doleful dumps; for to church they must go, and yet it looked as if they should never get there. So at last the Sheriff said that yonder, in the golden hut in the grove, lived a maiden, and if they could only get the loan of her calf—

"I know it can drag the coach, though it were as heavy as a mountain."

Well, they all thought it would look silly to be drawn to church by a calf, but there was no help for it, so they had to send a third time, and ask so prettily in the King's name, if he couldn't get the loan of the calf the Sheriff had spoken of, and the Mastermaid let them have it on the spot, for she was not going to say "no" this time either. So they put the calf on before the horses, and waited to see if it would do any good, and away went the coach over high and low, and stock and stone, so that they could scarce draw their breath; sometimes they were on the ground, and sometimes up in the air, and when they reached the church, the calf began to run round and round it like a spinning-wheel, so that they had hard work to get out of the coach, and into the church. When they went back, it was the same story, only they went faster, and they reached the palace almost before they knew they had set out.

Now when they sat down to dinner, the Prince who had served with the Giant said he thought they ought to ask the maiden who had lent them her shovel-handle and porch-door, and calf, to come up to the palace.

"For," said he, "if we hadn't got these three things, we should have been sticking here still."

Yes; the King thought that only fair and right, so he sent five of his best men down to the golden hut to greet the maiden from the King, and to ask her if she wouldn't be so good as to come up and dine at the palace.

"Greet the King from me," said the Mastermaid, "and tell him, if he's too good to come to me, so am I too good to go to him."

So the King had to go himself, and then the Mastermaid went up with him without more ado; and as the King thought she was more than she seemed to be, he sat her down in the highest seat by the side of the youngest bridegroom.

Now, when they had sat a little while at table, the Mastermaid took out her golden apple, and the golden cock and hen, which she had carried off from the Giant, and put them down on the table before her, and the cock and hen began at once to peck at one another, and to fight for the golden apple.

"Oh! only look," said the Prince; "see how those two strive for the apple."

"Yes!" said the Mastermaid; "so we two strove to get away that time when we were together in the hill-side."

Then the spell was broken, and the Prince knew her again, and you may fancy how glad he was. But as for the witch who had rolled the apple over to him, he had her torn to pieces between twenty-four horses, so that there was not a bit of her left, and after that they held on with the wedding in real earnest; and though they were still stiff and footsore, the Constable, the Attorney, and the Sheriff, kept it up with the best of them.

Boots Who Made the
Princess Say, "That's a Story"

ONCE ON a time there was a king who had a daughter, and she was such a dreadful story-teller that the like of her was not to be found far nor near. So the king gave out, that if any one could tell such a string of lies as would get her to say, "That's a story," he should have her to wife, and half the kingdom besides. Well, many came, as you may fancy, to try their luck, for every one would have been very glad to have the Princess, to say nothing of the kingdom; but they all cut a sorry figure, for the Princess was so given to story-telling, that all their lies went in at one ear and out of the other. Among the rest came three brothers to try their luck, and the two elder went first, but they fared no better than those who had gone before them. Last of all, the third, Boots, set off and found the Princess in the farm-yard.

"Good morning," he said, "and thank you for nothing."

"Good morning," said she, "and the same to you."

Then she went on—

"You haven't such a fine farm-yard as ours, I'll be bound; for when two shepherds stand, one at each end of it, and blow their ram's horns, the one can't hear the other."

"Haven't we though!" answered Boots; "ours is far bigger; for when a cow begins to go with calf at one end of it, she doesn't get to the other end before the time to drop her calf is come."

"I dare say!" said the Princess. "Well, but you haven't such a big ox, after all, as ours yonder; for when two men

41

sit, one on each horn, they can't touch each other with a twenty-foot pole."

"Stuff!" said Boots; "is that all? why, we have an ox who is so big, that when two men sit, one on each horn, and each blows his great mountain-trumpet, they can't hear one another."

"I dare say," said the Princess; "but you haven't so much milk as we, I'll be bound; for we milk our cows into great pails, and carry them in-doors, and empty them into great tubs, and so we make great, great cheeses."

"Oh! you do, do you?" said Boots. "Well, we milk ours into great tubs, and then we put them in carts and drive them in-doors, and then we turn them out into great brewing vats, and so we make cheeses as big as a great house. We had, too, a dun mare to tread the cheese well together when it was making; but once she tumbled down into the cheese, and we lost her; and after we had eaten at this cheese seven years, we came upon a dun mare, alive and kicking. Well, once after that I was going to drive this mare to the mill, and her back-bone snapped in two; but I wasn't put out, not I, for I took a spruce sapling, and put it into her for a back-bone, and she had no other back-bone all the while we had her. But the sapling grew up into such a tall tree, that I climbed right up to heaven by it, and when I got there, I saw the Virgin Mary sitting and spinning the foam of the sea into pigs'-bristle ropes; but just then the spruce-fir broke short off, and I couldn't get down again; so the Virgin Mary let me down by one of the ropes, and down I slipped straight into a fox's hole, and who should sit there but my mother and your father cobbling shoes; and just as I stepped in, my mother gave your father such a box on the ear, that it made his whiskers curl."

"That's a story!" said the Princess; "my father never did any such a thing in all his born days!"

So Boots got the Princess to wife, and half the kingdom besides.

Dapplegrim

ONCE ON a time there was a rich couple who had twelve sons; but the youngest when he was grown up said he wouldn't stay any longer at home, but be off into the world to try his luck. His father and mother said he did very well at home, and had better stay where he was. But no, he couldn't rest; away he must and would go. So at last they gave him leave. And when he had walked a good bit, he came to a king's palace, where he asked for a place and got it.

Now the daughter of the king of that land had been carried off into the hill by a Troll, and the king had no other children; so he and all his land were in great grief and sorrow, and the king gave his word that any one who could set her free should have the Princess and half the kingdom. But there was no one who could do it, though many tried.

So when the lad had been there a year or so, he longed to go home again and see his father and mother, and back he went; but when he got home his father and mother were dead, and his brothers had shared all that the old people owned between them, and so there was nothing left for the lad.

"Shan't I have anything at all, then, out of father's and mother's goods?" said the lad.

"Who could tell you were still alive, when you went gossiping and wandering about so long?" said his brothers. "But all the same; there are twelve mares up on the hill which we haven't yet shared among us; if you choose to take them for your share, you're quite welcome."

Yes, the lad was quite content; so he thanked his brothers, and went at once up on the hill, where the twelve mares were grazing. And when he got up there and found them, each of them had a foal at her side, and one of them had besides, along with her, a big dapple-gray foal, which was so sleek that the sun shone from its coat.

"A fine fellow you are, my little foal," said the lad.

"Yes," said the Foal; "but if you'll only kill all the other foals, so that I may run and nurse from all the mares one year more, you'll see how big and sleek I'll be then."

Yes, the lad was ready to do that; so he killed all those twelve foals, and went home again.

So when he came back the next year to look after his foal and mares, the foal was so fat and sleek, that the sun shone from its coat, and it had grown so big, the lad had hard work to mount it. As for the mares, they had each of them another foal.

"Well, it's quite plain I lost nothing by letting you nurse from all my twelve mares," said the lad to the yearling, "but now you're big enough to come along with me."

"No," said the Colt, "I must stay here a year longer, and now kill all the twelve foals, that I may nurse from all the mares this year, too, and you'll see how big and sleek I'll be by summer."

Yes, the lad did that; and next year when he went up on the hill to look after his colt and the mares, each mare had her foal, but the dapple colt was so tall the lad couldn't reach up to his crest when he wanted to feel how fat he was; and so sleek he was too, that his coat glistened in the sunshine.

"Big and beautiful you were last year, my colt," said the lad, "but this year you're far grander. There's no such horse in the king's stable. But now you must come along with me."

"No," said Dapple again, "I must stay here one year more. Kill the twelve foals as before, that I may nurse from the mares the whole year, and then just come and look at me when the summer comes."

Yes, the lad did that; he killed the foals, and went away home.

But when he went up next year to look after Dapple and the mares, he was quite astonished. So tall, and stout, and sturdy, he never thought a horse could be; for Dapple had to lie down on all fours before the lad could mount him, and it was hard work to get up even then, although he lay flat; and his coat was so smooth and sleek, the sunbeams shone from it as from a looking-glass.

This time Dapple was willing enough to follow the lad, so he jumped up on his back, and when he came riding home to his brothers, they all clapped their hands and crossed themselves, for such a horse they had never heard of nor seen before.

"If you will only get me the best shoes you can for my horse, and the grandest saddle and bridle that are to be found," said the lad, "you may have my twelve mares that graze up on the hill yonder, and their twelve foals into the bargain." For you must know that this year too every mare had her foal.

Yes, his brothers were ready to do that, and so the lad got such strong shoes under his horse, that the stones flew high aloft as he rode away across the hills; and he had a golden saddle and a golden bridle, which gleamed and glistened a long way off.

"Now we're off to the king's palace," said Dapplegrim— that was his name; "but mind you ask the king for a good stable and good fodder for me."

Yes, the lad said he would mind; he'd be sure not to forget; and when he rode off from his brothers' house, you may be sure it wasn't long, with such a horse under him, before he got to the king's palace.

When he came there, the king was standing on the steps, and stared and stared at the man who came riding along.

"Nay, nay!" said he, "such a man and such a horse I never yet saw in all my life."

But when the lad asked if he could get a place in the king's household, the king was so glad he was ready to jump and dance as he stood on the steps.

Well, they said, perhaps he might get a place there.

"Ay," said the lad, "but I must have good stable-room for my horse, and fodder that one can trust."

Yes, he should have meadow-hay and oats, as much as Dapple could cram, and all the other knights had to lead their horses out of the stable, that Dapplegrim might stand alone, and have it all to himself.

But it wasn't long before all the others in the king's household began to be jealous of the lad, and there was no end to the bad things they would have done to him, if they had only dared. At last they thought of telling the king he had said he was man enough to set the king's daughter free—whom the Troll had long since carried away into the hill—if he only chose. The king called the lad before him, and said he had heard the lad said he was good to do so and so; so now he must go and do it. If he did it he knew how the king had promised his daughter and half the kingdom, and that promise would be faithfully kept; if he didn't, he should be killed.

The lad kept on saying he never said any such thing; but it was no good,—the king wouldn't even listen to him; and so the end of it was he was forced to say he'd go and try.

So he went into the stable, down in the mouth and heavy-hearted, and then Dapplegrim asked him at once why he was in such dumps.

Then the lad told him all, and how he couldn't tell which way to turn—

"For as for setting the Princess free, that's downright nonsense."

"Oh! but it might be done, perhaps," said Dapplegrim. "I'll help you though; but you must first have me well shod. You must go and ask for ten pound of iron and twelve pound of steel for the shoes, and one smith to hammer and another to hold."

Yes, the lad did that, and got for answer "Yes!" He got both the iron and the steel, and the smiths, and so Dapplegrim was shod both strong and well, and off went the lad from the courtyard in a cloud of dust.

But when he came to the hill into which the Princess had been carried, the pinch was how to get up the steep wall of rock where the Troll's cave was in which the Princess had been hid. For you must know the hill stood straight up and down right on end, as upright as a house-wall, and as smooth as a sheet of glass.

The first time the lad went at it he got a little way up; but then Dapple's fore-legs slipped, and down they went again, with a sound like thunder on the hill.

The second time he rode at it he got some way farther up; but then one fore-leg slipped, and down they went with a crash like a landslide.

But the third time Dapple said,—

"Now we must show our courage;" and went at it again till the stones flew heaven-high about them, and so they got up.

Then the lad rode right into the cave at full speed, and caught up the Princess, and threw her over his saddle, and out and down again before the Troll had time even to get on his legs; and so the Princess was freed.

When the lad came back to the palace, the king was both happy and glad to get his daughter back; that you may well believe; but somehow or other, though I don't know how, the others about the court had so brought it about that the king was angry with the lad after all.

"Thanks you shall have for freeing my Princess," said he to the lad, when he brought the Princess into the hall, and made his bow.

"She ought to be mine as well as yours; for you're an honest man, I hope," said the lad.

"Ay, ay!" said the king, "have her you shall, since I said it; but, first of all, you must make the sun shine into my palace hall."

Now, you must know there was a high steep ridge of rock close outside the windows, which threw such a shade over the hall that never a sunbeam shone into it.

"That wasn't in our bargain," answered the lad; "but I see this is past praying against; I must even go and try my luck, for the Princess I must and will have."

So down he went to Dapple, and told him what the king wanted, and Dapplegrim thought it might easily be done, but first of all he must be new shod; and for that ten pound of iron, and twelve pound of steel besides, were needed, and two smiths, one to hammer and the other to hold, and then they'd soon get the sun to shine into the palace hall.

So when the lad asked for all these things, he got them at once—the king couldn't say nay for very shame; and so Dapplegrim got new shoes, and such shoes! Then the lad jumped upon his back, and off they went again; and for every leap that Dapplegrim gave, down sunk the ridge fifteen yards into the earth, and so they went on till there was nothing left of the ridge for the king to see.

When the lad got back to the king's palace he asked the king if the Princess were not his now; for now no one could say that the sun didn't shine into the hall. But then the others set the king's back up again, and he answered the lad should have her of course, he had never thought of anything else; but first of all he must get as grand a horse for the bride to ride on to church as the bridegroom had himself.

The lad said the king hadn't spoken a word about this before, and that he thought he had now fairly earned the Princess; but the king held to his own; and more, if the lad couldn't do that he should lose his life; that was what the king said. So the lad went down to the stable in doleful dumps, as you may well fancy, and there he told Dapplegrim all about it; how the king had laid that task on him, to find the bride as good a horse as the bridegroom had himself, else he would lose his life.

"But that's not so easy," he said, "for your match isn't to be found in the wide world."

"Oh yes, I have a match," said Dapplegrim; "but 'tisn't so easy to find him, for he abides in Hell. Still we'll try. And now you must go up to the king and ask for new shoes for me, ten pound of iron, and twelve pound of steel; and two smiths, one to hammer and one to hold; and mind you see that the points and ends of these shoes are sharp; and twelve sacks of rye, and twelve sacks of barley, and twelve slaughtered oxen, we must have with us; and mind, we must have the twelve ox-hides, with twelve hundred spikes driven into each; and, let me see, a big tar-barrel;——that's all we want."

So the lad went up to the king and asked for all that Dapplegrim had said, and the king again thought he couldn't say nay, for shame's sake, and so the lad got all he wanted.

Well, he jumped up on Dapplegrim's back, and rode away from the palace, and when he had ridden far far over hill and heath, Dapple asked,—

"Do you hear anything?"

"Yes, I hear an awful hissing and rustling up in the air," said the lad; "I think I'm getting afraid."

"That's all the wild birds that fly through the wood. They are sent to stop us; but just cut a hole in the corn-sacks, and then they'll have so much to do with the corn, they'll forget us quite."

Yes, the lad did that; he cut holes in the corn-sacks, so that the rye and barley ran out on all sides. Then all the wild birds that were in the wood came flying round them so thick that the sunbeams grew dark; but as soon as they saw the corn, they couldn't keep to their purpose, but flew down and began to pick and scratch at the rye and barley, and after that they began to fight among themselves. As for Dapplegrim and the lad, they forgot all about them, and did them no harm.

So the lad rode on and on—far far over mountain and dale, over sand-hills and moor. Then Dapplegrim began to prick up his ears again, and at last he asked the lad if he heard anything.

"Yes; now I hear such an ugly roaring and howling in the wood all round, it makes me quite afraid."

"Ah!" said Dapplegrim, "that's all the wild beasts that range through the wood, and they're sent out to stop us. But just cast out the twelve slaughtered oxen, that will give them enough to do, and so they'll forget us outright."

Yes, the lad cast out the oxen, and then all the wild beasts in the wood, both bears, and wolves, and lions—all fierce beasts of all kinds—came after them. But when they saw the oxen, they began to fight for them among themselves, till blood flowed in streams; but Dapplegrim and the lad they quite forgot.

So the lad rode far away, and they changed the landscape many many times, for Dapplegrim didn't let the grass grow under him, as you may fancy. At last Dapple gave a great neigh.

"Do you hear anything?" he said.

"Yes, I hear something like a colt neighing loud, a long long way off," answered the lad.

"That's a full-grown colt then," said Dapplegrim, "if we hear him neigh so loud such a long way off."

After that they travelled a good bit, changing the landscape once or twice maybe. Then Dapplegrim gave another neigh.

"Now listen, and tell me if you hear anything," he said.

"Yes, now I hear a neigh like a full-grown horse," answered the lad.

"Ay! ay!" said Dapplegrim, "you'll hear him once again soon, and then you'll hear he's got a voice of his own."

So they travelled on and on, and changed the landscape once or twice perhaps, and then Dapplegrim neighed the third time; but before he could ask the lad if he heard anything, something gave such a neigh across the wild hill-side, the lad thought hill and rock would surely be broken to pieces.

"Now he's here!" said Dapplegrim; "make haste, now, and throw the ox-hides, with the spikes in them over me, and throw down the tar-barrel on the plain; then climb up into that great spruce tree yonder. When it comes, fire will flash out of both nostrils, and then the tar-barrel will catch fire. Now, mind what I say. If the flame rises—I win; if it falls, I lose; but if you see me winning, take and cast the bridle—you must take it off me—over its head, and then it will be tame enough."

So just as the lad had done throwing the ox-hides, with the spikes, over Dapplegrim, and had cast down the tar-barrel on the plain, and had got well up into the spruce tree, up galloped a horse, with fire flashing out of his nostrils, and the flame caught the tar-barrel at once. Then Dapplegrim and the strange horse began to fight till the stones flew heaven-high. They fought, and bit, and kicked both with fore-feet and hind-feet, and sometimes the lad could see them, and sometimes he couldn't, but at last the flame began to rise; for wherever the strange horse kicked or bit, he met the spiked hides, and at last he had to give in. When the lad saw that, he wasn't long in getting down from the tree, and in throwing the bridle over its head, and then it was so tame you could hold it with a length of twine.

And what do you think? that horse was dappled too, and so like Dapplegrim, you couldn't tell which was which. Then the lad mounted the new Dapple he had broken, and rode home to the palace, and old Dapplegrim ran loose by his side. So when he got home, there stood the king out in the yard.

"Can you tell me now," said the lad, "which is the horse I have caught and broken, and which is the one I had before. If you can't, I think your daughter is fairly mine."

Then the king went and looked at both Dapples, high and low, before and behind, but there wasn't a hair on one which wasn't on the other as well.

"No," said the king, "that I can't; and since you've got my daughter such a grand horse for her wedding, you shall have her with all my heart. But still we'll have one trial more, just to see whether you're fated to have her. First, she shall hide herself twice, and then you shall hide yourself twice. If you can find out her hiding-place, and she can't find out yours, why then, you're fated to have her, and so you shall have her."

"That's not in the bargain either," said the lad; "but we must just try, since it must be so," and so the Princess went off to hide herself first.

So she turned herself into a duck, and lay swimming on a pond that was close to the palace. But the lad only ran down to the stable, and asked Dapplegrim what she had done with herself.

"Oh, you only need to take your gun," said Dapplegrim, "and go down to the edge of the pond, and aim at the duck which lies swimming about there, and she'll soon show herself."

So the lad snatched up his gun and ran off to the pond. "I'll just take a pop at this duck," he said, and began to aim at it.

"Nay, nay, dear friend, don't shoot. It's I," said the Princess.

So he had found her once.

The second time the Princess turned herself into a loaf of bread, and laid herself on the table among four other loaves; and so like was she to the others, no one could say which was which.

But the lad went again down to the stable to Dapplegrim, and said how the Princess had hidden herself again, and he couldn't tell at all what had become of her.

"Oh, just take and sharpen a good bread-knife," said Dapplegrim, "and do as if you were going to cut in two the third loaf on the left hand of those four loaves which are lying on the table in the king's kitchen, and you'll find her soon enough."

Yes, the lad was down in the kitchen in no time, and began to sharpen the biggest bread-knife he could lay hands on; then he caught hold of the third loaf on the left hand, and put the knife to it, as though he was going to cut it in two.

"I'll just have a slice off this loaf," he said.

"Nay, dear friend," said the Princess, "don't cut. It's I."

So he had found her twice.

Then he was to go and hide; but he and Dapplegrim had settled it all so well beforehand, it wasn't easy to find him. First he turned himself into a tick and hid himself in Dapplegrim's left nostril; and the Princess went about hunting him everywhere, high and low; at last she wanted to go into Dapplegrim's stall, but he began to bite and kick, so that she daren't go near him, and so she couldn't find the lad.

"Well," she said, "since I can't find you, you must show where you are yourself"; and in a flash the lad stood there on the stable floor.

The second time Dapplegrim told him again what to do; and then he turned himself into a clod of earth, and stuck himself between Dapplegrim's hoof and shoe on the near forefoot. So the Princess hunted up and down, out and in, everywhere; at last she came into the stable, and wanted to go into Dapplegrim's stall. This time he let her come up to him, and she searched high and low, but under his hoofs she couldn't come, for he stood firm as a rock on his feet, and so she couldn't find the lad.

"Well; you must just show yourself, for I'm sure I can't find you," said the Princess, and as she spoke the lad stood by her side on the stable floor.

"Now you are mine indeed," said the lad; "for now you can see I'm fated to have you." This he said both to the father and daughter.

"Yes; it is so fated," said the king; "so it must be."

Then they got ready the wedding in right-down earnest, and lost no time about it; and the lad got on Dapplegrim, and the Princess on Dapplegrim's match, and then you may fancy they were not long on their way to the church.

Tatterhood

ONCE ON a time there was a king and a queen who had no children, and that gave the queen much grief; she scarce had one happy hour. She was always bewailing and bemoaning herself, and saying how dull and lonesome it was in the palace.

"If we had children there'd be life enough," she said.

Wherever she went in all her realm she found God's blessing in children, even in the vilest hut; and wherever she came she heard the housewives scolding the children, and saying how they had done that and that wrong. All this the queen heard, and thought it would be so nice to do as other women did. At last the king and queen took into their palace a stranger lassie to rear up, that they might have her always with them, to love her if she did well, and scold her if she did wrong, like their own child.

So one day the little lassie whom they had taken as their own, ran down into the palace-yard, and was playing with a gold apple. Just then an old beggar wife came by, who had a little girl with her, and it wasn't long before the little lassie and the beggar's child were great friends, and began to play together, and to toss the gold apple about between them. When the Queen saw this, as she sat at a window in the palace, she tapped on the pane for her foster-daughter to come up. She went at once, but the beggar-girl went up too; and as they went into the Queen's bower, each held the other by the hand. Then the Queen began to scold the little lady, and to say——

"You ought to be above running about and playing with a tattered beggar's brat."

And so she wanted to drive the lassie down-stairs.

"If the Queen only knew my mother's power, she'd not

54

drive me out," said the little lassie; and when the Queen asked what she meant more plainly, she told her how her mother could get her children if she chose. The Queen wouldn't believe it, but the lassie held her own, and said every word of it was true, and told the Queen only to try and make her mother do it. So the Queen sent the lassie down to fetch up her mother.

"Do you know what your daughter says?" asked the Queen of the old woman, as soon as ever she came into the room.

No; the beggar-wife knew nothing about it.

"Well, she says you can get me children if you will," answered the Queen.

"Queens shouldn't listen to beggar-lassies' silly stories," said the old wife, and strode out of the room.

Then the Queen got angry, and wanted again to drive out the little lassie; but she declared it was true every word that she had said.

"Let the Queen only give my mother a drop to drink," said the lassie; "when she gets merry she'll soon find out a way to help you."

The Queen was ready to try this; so the beggar-wife was fetched up again once more, and treated both with wine and mead as much as she chose; and so it was not long before her tongue began to wag. Then the Queen came out again with the same question she had asked before.

"One way to help you perhaps I know," said the beggar-wife. "Your Majesty must make them bring in two pails of water some evening before you go to bed. In each of them you must wash yourself, and afterwards throw away the water under the bed. When you look under the bed next morning, two flowers will have sprung up, one fair and one ugly. The fair one you must eat, the ugly one you must let stand; but mind you don't forget the last."

That was what the beggar-wife said.

Yes; the Queen did what the beggar-wife advised her to do; and she had the water brought up in two pails, washed herself in them, and emptied them under the bed;

and lo! when she looked under the bed next morning, there stood two flowers; one was ugly and foul, and had black leaves; but the other was so bright, and fair, and lovely, she had never seen its like; so she ate it up at once. But the pretty flower tasted so sweet, that she couldn't help herself. She ate the other up too, for, she thought, "it can't hurt or help one much either way, I'll be bound."

Well, sure enough, after a while the Queen was brought to bed. First of all, she had a girl who had a wooden spoon in her hand, and rode upon a goat; ugly she was, and the very moment she came into the world she bawled out "Mamma."

"If I'm your mamma," said the Queen, "God give me grace to mend your ways."

"Oh, don't be sorry," said the girl, who rode on the goat, "for one will soon come after me who is better looking."

So, after a while, the Queen had another girl, who was so fair and sweet, no one had ever set eyes on such a lovely child, and with her you may fancy the Queen was very well pleased. The elder twin they called "Tatterhood," because she was always so ugly and ragged, and because she had a hood which hung about her ears in tatters. The Queen could scarce bear to look at her, and the nurses tried to shut her up in a room by herself, but it was all no good; where the younger twin was, there she must also be, and no one could ever keep them apart.

Well, one Christmas eve, when they were half grown up, there rose such a frightful noise and clatter in the gallery outside the Queen's bedroom. So Tatterhood asked what it was that dashed and crashed so out in the passage.

"Oh!" said the Queen, "it isn't worth asking about."

But Tatterhood wouldn't give over till she found out all about it; and so the Queen told her it was a pack of Trolls and witches who had come there to keep Christmas. So Tatterhood said she'd just go out and drive them away; and in spite of all they could say, and however much they begged and prayed her to let the Trolls alone, she must and would go out to drive the witches off; but she begged the Queen to mind and keep all the doors close shut, so that not one of them came so much as the least bit open. Having said this, off she went with her wooden spoon, and began to hunt and sweep away the hags; and all this while there was such a commotion out in the gallery, the like of it was never heard. The whole palace creaked and groaned as if every joint and beam were going to be torn out of its place. Now, how it was, I'm sure I can't tell; but somehow or other one door did get the least bit open, then her twin sister just peeped out to see how things were going with Tatterhood, and put her head a tiny bit through the opening. But, POP! up came an old witch, and whipped off her head, and stuck a calf's head on her shoulders instead; and so the Princess ran back into the room on all-fours, and began to "moo" like a calf. When Tatterhood came back and saw her sister, she scolded them all round, and was very angry because they hadn't kept better watch, and asked them what they thought of their carelessness now, when her sister was turned into a calf.

"But still I'll see if I can't set her free," she said.

Then she asked the King for a ship that was ready to sail, and well fitted with stores; but captain and sailors she wouldn't have. No; she would sail away with her sister all alone; and there was no holding her back, at last they let her have her own way.

Then Tatterhood sailed off, and steered her ship right under the land where the witches dwelt, and when she came to the landing-place, she told her sister to stay quite still on board the ship; but she herself rode on her goat up to the witches' castle. When she got there, one of the windows in the gallery was open, and there she saw her sister's head hung up on the window frame; so she leapt her goat through the window into the gallery, snapped up the head, and set off with it. After her came the witches to try to get the head again, and they flocked about her as thick as a swarm of bees or a nest of ants; but the goat snorted and puffed, and butted with his horns, and

Tatterhood beat and banged them about with her wooden spoon; and so the pack of witches had to give it up. So Tatterhood got back to her ship, took the calf's head off her sister, and put her own on again, and then she became a girl as she had been before. After that she sailed a long, long way, to a strange king's realm.

Now the king of that land was a widower, and had an only son. So when he saw the strange sail, he sent messengers down to the strand to find out whence it came, and who owned it; but when the king's men came down there, they saw never a living soul on board but Tatterhood, and there she was, riding round and round the deck on her goat at full speed, till her wild hair streamed again in the wind. The folk from the palace were all amazed at this sight, and asked were there not more on board. Yes, there were; she had a sister with her, said Tatterhood. Her, too, they wanted to see, but Tatterhood said "No,"

"No one shall see her, unless the King come himself," she said; and so she began to gallop about on her goat till the deck thundered again.

So when the servants got back to the palace, and told what they had seen and heard down at the ship, the King was for setting out at once, that he might see the lassie that rode on the goat. When he got down, Tatterhood led out her sister, and she was so fair and gentle, the King fell over head and ears in love with her as he stood. He brought them both back with him to the palace, and wanted to have the sister for his queen; but Tatterhood said "No"; the King couldn't have her in any way, unless the King's son chose to have Tatterhood. That you may fancy the Prince was very reluctant to do, such an ugly girl as Tatterhood was; but at last the king and all the others in the palace talked him into it, and he agreed, giving his word to take her for his queen; but it went sore against his wishes, and he was an unhappy man.

Now they set about the wedding, both with brewing and baking; and when all was ready, they were to go to church;

but the Prince thought it the weariest ride to church he had ever had in all his life. First, the King drove off with his bride, and she was so lovely and so grand, all the people stopped to look after her all along the road, and they stared at her till she was out of sight. After them came the Prince on horseback by the side of Tatterhood, who trotted along on her goat with her wooden spoon in her fist, and to look at him, it was more like going to a burial than a wedding, and that his own; so sorrowful he seemed, and with never a word to say.

"Why don't you talk?" asked Tatterhood, when they had ridden a bit.

"Why, what should I talk about?" answered the Prince.

"Well, you might at least ask me why I ride upon this ugly goat," said Tatterhood.

"Why do you ride on that ugly goat?" asked the Prince.

"Is it an ugly goat? why, it's the grandest horse a bride ever rode on," answered Tatterhood; and in a flash the goat became a horse, and that the finest the Prince had ever set eyes on.

Then they rode on again a bit, but the Prince was just as unhappy as before, and couldn't get a word out. So Tatterhood asked him again why he didn't talk, and when the Prince answered, he didn't know what to talk about, she said—

"You can at least ask me why I ride with this ugly spoon in my fist."

"Why do you ride with that ugly spoon?" asked the Prince.

"Is it an ugly spoon? why, it's the loveliest silver wand a bride ever bore," said Tatterhood; and in a flash it became a silver wand, so dazzling bright, the sunbeams glistened from it.

So they rode on another bit, but the Prince was just as sorrowful, and said never a word. In a little while Tatterhood asked him again why he didn't talk, and told him to ask why she wore that ugly gray hood on her head.

"Why do you wear that ugly gray hood on your head?" asked the Prince.

"Is it an ugly hood? why, it's the brightest golden crown a bride ever wore," answered Tatterhood, and it became a crown on the spot.

Now they rode on a long while again, and the Prince was so unhappy, that he sat without sound or speech, just as before. So his bride asked him again why he didn't talk, and told him to ask now why her face was so ugly and ashen-gray?"

"Ah!" asked the Prince, "why is your face so ugly and ashen-gray?"

"I ugly," said the bride; "you think my sister pretty, but I am ten times prettier"; and lo! when the Prince looked at her, she was so lovely, he thought there never was so lovely a woman in all the world. After that, I shouldn't wonder if the Prince found his tongue, and no longer rode along hanging down his head.

So they drank the bridal cup both deep and long, and, after that, both Prince and King set out with their brides to the Princess's father's palace, and there they had another bridal feast, and drank anew, both deep and long. There was no end to the fun; and, if you make haste and run to the King's palace, I dare say you'll find there's still a drop of the bridal ale left for you.

Soria Moria Castle

ONCE ON a time there was a poor couple who had a son whose name was Halvor. Ever since he was a little boy he would turn his hand to nothing, but just sat there and groped about in the ashes. His father and mother often put him out to learn this trade or that, but Halvor could stay nowhere; for, when he had been there a day or two, he ran away from his master, and never stopped till he was sitting again in the fireplace, poking about in the cinders.

Well, one day a skipper came and asked Halvor if he hadn't a mind to be with him, and go to sea, and see strange lands. Yes, Halvor would like that very much; so he wasn't long in getting himself ready.

How long they sailed I'm sure I can't tell; but the end of it was, they fell into a great storm, and when it was blown over, and it got still again, they couldn't tell where they were; for they had been driven away to a strange coast, which none of them knew anything about.

Well, as there was just no wind at all, they stayed lying wind-bound there, and Halvor asked the skipper's leave to go on shore and look about him; he would sooner go, he said, than lie there and sleep.

"Do you think now you're fit to show yourself before folk," said the skipper, "why, you've no clothes than those rags you stand in?"

But Halvor stuck to his own, and so at last he got leave, but he was to be sure and come back as soon as ever it began to blow. So off he went and found a lovely land; wherever he came there were fine large flat corn-fields and rich meads, but he couldn't catch a glimpse of a living soul. Well, it began to blow, but Halvor thought he hadn't seen enough yet, and he wanted to walk a little farther, just to see if he couldn't meet any folk. So after a while he came to a broad high road, so smooth and even, you might easily roll an egg along it. Halvor followed this, and when evening drew on he saw a great castle ever so far off, from which the sunbeams shone. So as he had now walked the whole day and hadn't taken a bit to eat with him, he was as hungry as a hunter, but still the nearer he came to the castle, the more afraid he got.

In the castle kitchen a great fire was blazing, and Halvor went into it, but such a kitchen he had never seen in all his born days. It was so grand and fine; there were vessels of silver and vessels of gold, but still never a living soul. So when Halvor had stood there a while and no one came out, he went and opened a door, and there inside sat a Princess who spun upon a spinning-wheel.

"Nay, nay, now!" she called out, "dare Christian folk come hither? But now you'd best be off about your business, if you don't want the Troll to gobble you up; for here lives a Troll with three heads."

"All one to me," said the lad, "I'd be just as glad to hear he had four heads beside; I'd like to see what kind of fellow he is. As for going, I won't go at all. I've done no harm; but meat you must get me, for I'm almost starved to death."

When Halvor had eaten his fill, the Princess told him to try if he could swing the sword that hung against the wall; no, he couldn't swing it, he couldn't even lift it up.

"Oh!" said the Princess, "now you must go and take a sip from that flask that hangs by its side; that's what the Troll does every time he goes out to use the sword."

So Halvor took a pull, and in the twinkling of an eye he could swing the sword like nothing; and now he thought it high time the Troll came; and lo! just then up came the Troll puffing and blowing. Halvor jumped behind the door.

"HUTETU," said the Troll, as he put his head in at the door, "what a smell of Christian man's blood!"

"Ay," said Halvor, "you'll soon know that to your cost," and with that he chopped off all his heads.

Now the Princess was so glad that she was free, she both danced and sang, but then all at once she called her sisters to mind, and so she said,—

"Would my sisters were free too!"

"Where are they?" asked Halvor.

Well, she told him all about it; one was taken away by a Troll to his castle, which lay fifty miles off, and the other by another Troll to his castle, which was fifty miles farther still.

"But now," she said, "you must first help me to get this ugly Troll's body out of the house."

Yes, Halvor was so strong he swept everything away, and made it all clean and tidy in no time. So they had a good and happy time of it, and next morning he set off at peep of gray dawn; he could take no rest by the way, but ran and walked the whole day. When he first saw the castle he got a little afraid; it was far grander than the first, but here too there wasn't a living soul to be seen. So Halvor went into the kitchen, and didn't stop there either, but went straight farther on into the house.

"Nay, nay," called out the Princess, "dare Christian folk come hither? I don't know I'm sure how long it is since I came here, but in all that time I haven't seen a Christian man. 'Twere best you saw how to get away as fast as you came; for here lives a Troll who has six heads."

"I shan't go," said Halvor, "if he had six heads besides."

"He'll take you up and swallow you down alive," said the Princess.

But it was no good, Halvor wouldn't go; he wasn't at all afraid of the Troll, but meat and drink he must have, for he was half starved after his long journey. Well, he got as much of that as he wished, but then the Princess wanted him to be off again.

"No," said Halvor, "I won't go, I've done no harm, and I've nothing to be afraid about."

"He won't stay to ask that," said the Princess, "for he'll take you without law or leave; but as you won't go, just try if you can swing that sword yonder, which the Troll wields in war."

He couldn't swing it, and then the Princess said he must take a sip from the flask which hung by its side, and when he had done that he could swing it.

Just then back came the Troll, and he was both stout and big, so that he had to go sideways to get through the door. When the Troll got his first head in he called out—

"HUTETU, what a smell of Christian man's blood!"

But that very moment Halvor chopped off his first head, and so on all the rest as they popped in. The Princess was overjoyed, but just then she came to think of her sisters, and wished out loud they were free. Halvor thought that might easily be done, and wanted to be off at once, but first he had to help the Princess to get the Troll's body out of the way, and so he could only set out next morning.

It was a long way to the castle, and he had to walk fast and run hard to reach it in time; but about nightfall he saw the castle, which was far finer and grander than either of the others. This time he wasn't the least afraid, but walked straight through the kitchen, and into the castle. There sat a Princess who was so pretty, there was no end to her loveliness. She, too, like the others, told him there hadn't been Christian folk there ever since she came thither, and told him go away again, else the Troll would swallow him alive, and do you know, she said, he has nine heads.

"Ay, ay," said Halvor, "if he had nine other heads, and nine other heads still, I won't go away," and so he stood fast before the stove. The Princess kept on begging him so prettily to go away, lest the Troll should gobble him up, but Halvor said—

"Let him come as soon as he likes."

So she gave him the Troll's sword, and told him take a sip from the flask, that he might be able to swing and wield it.

Just then back came the Troll puffing and blowing and tearing along. He was far stouter and bigger than the other two, and he too had to go on one side to get through the door. So when he got his first head in, he said as the others had said—

"HUTETU, what a smell of Christian man's blood!"

That very moment Halvor chopped off the first head and then all the rest; but the last was the toughest of them all, and it was the hardest bit of work Halvor had to do to get it chopped off, although he knew very well he had strength enough to do it.

So all the Princesses came together to that castle, which was called *Soria Moria Castle,* and they were glad and happy as they had never been in all their lives before, and they all were fond of Halvor and Halvor of them, and he might choose the one he liked best for his bride; but the youngest was fondest of him of all the three.

But there, after a while, Halvor went about, and was so strange and dull and silent. Then the Princesses asked him what he lacked, and if he didn't like to live with them any longer? Yes, he did, for they had enough and to spare, and he was well off in every way, but still somehow or other he did so long to go home, for his father and mother were alive, and them he had such a great wish to see.

Well, they thought that might be done easily enough.

"You shall go thither and come back hither, safe and unharmed, if you will only follow our advice," said the Princesses.

Yes, he'd be sure to mind all they said. So they dressed him up till he was as grand as a king's son, and then they set a ring on his finger, and that was such a ring, he could wish himself thither and hither with it; but they told him to be sure not to take it off, and not to name their names, for there would be an end of all his bravery, and then he'd never see them more.

"If I only stood at home I'd be glad," said Halvor; and it was done as he had wished. Then stood Halvor at his father's cottage door before he knew a word about it. Now it was about dusk at even, and so, when they saw such a grand stately lord walk in, the old couple got so afraid they began to bow and scrape. Then Halvor asked if he couldn't stay there, and have a lodging there that night. No; that he couldn't.

"We can't do it at all," they said, "for we haven't this thing or that thing which such a lord is used to have; 'twere best your lordship went up to the farm, no long way off, for you can see the chimneys, and there they have lots of everything."

Halvor wouldn't hear of it—he wanted to stop; but the old couple stuck to their own, that he had better go to the farmer's; there he would get both meat and drink; as for them, they hadn't even a chair to offer him to sit down on.

"No," said Halvor, "I won't go up there till to-morrow early, but let me just stay here to-night; worst come to the worst, I can sit in the chimney corner."

Well, they couldn't say anything against that; so Halvor sat down by the fireplace, and began to poke about in the ashes, just as he used to do when he lay at home in old days, and stretched his lazy bones.

Well, they chattered and talked about many things; and they told Halvor about this thing and that; and so he asked them if they never had any children.

"Yes, yes, they had once a lad whose name was Halvor, but they didn't know whither he had wandered; they couldn't even tell whether he were dead or alive."

"Couldn't it be me now?" said Halvor.

"Let me see; I could tell him well enough," said the old wife, and rose up. "Our Halvor was so lazy and dull, he never did a thing; and besides, he was so ragged, that one tatter took hold of the next tatter on him. No; there never was the making of such a fine fellow in him as you are, master."

A little while after the old wife went to the hearth to poke up the fire, and when the blaze fell on Halvor's face, just as when he was at home of old poking about in the ashes, she knew him at once.

"Ah! but is it you after all, Halvor?" she cried; and then there was such joy for the old couple, there was no end to it; and she was forced to tell how he had fared, and the old dame was so fond and proud of him, nothing would do but he must go up at once to the farmer's and show himself to the lassies, who had always looked down on him. And off she went first, and Halvor followed after. So, when she got up there, she told them all how her Halvor had come home again, and now they should only just see how grand he was, for, said she, "he looks like nothing but a king's son."

"All very fine," said the lassies, and tossed up their heads. "We'll be bound he's just the same beggarly, ragged boy he always was."

Just then in walked Halvor, and then the lassies were all so taken aback, they forgot their linens drying by the fire, where they were sitting mending their clothes, and ran out in their smocks. Well, when they were got back again, they were so shamefaced they scarce dared look at Halvor, towards whom they had always been proud and haughty.

"Ay, ay," said Halvor, "you always thought yourselves so pretty and neat, no one could come near you; but now you should just see the eldest Princess I have set free; against her you look just like milkmaids, and the midmost is prettier still; but the youngest, who is my sweetheart, she's fairer than both sun and moon. Would to Heaven she were only here," said Halvor, "then you'd see what you would see."

He had scarce uttered these words before there they stood, but then he felt so sorry, for now what they had said came into his mind. Up at the farm there was a great feast got ready for the Princesses, and much was made of them, but they wouldn't stop there.

"No; we want to go down to your father and mother," they said to Halvor; "and so we'll go out now and look about us."

So he went down with them, and they came to a great lake just outside the farm. Close by the water was such a lovely green bank; here the Princesses said they would sit and rest a while; they thought it so sweet to sit down and look over the water.

So they sat down there, and when they had sat a while, the youngest Princess said,—

"I may as well comb your hair a little, Halvor."

Yes, Halvor laid his head on her lap, and so she combed his bonny locks, and it wasn't long before Halvor fell fast asleep. Then she took the ring from his finger, and put another in its place; and so she said—

"Now hold me all together! and now would we were all in SORIA MORIA CASTLE."

So when Halvor woke up, he could very well tell that he had lost the Princesses, and began to weep and wail; and he was so downcast, they couldn't comfort him at all. In spite of all his father and mother said, he wouldn't stop there, but said farewell to them, and said he was safe not to see them again; for if he couldn't find the Princesses again, he thought it not worth while to live.

Well, he had still three hundred dollars left, so he put them into his pocket, and set out on his way. So when he had walked a while, he met a man with a fine horse, and he wanted to buy it, and began to bargain with the man.

"Ay," said the man, "to tell the ruth, I never thought of selling him; but if we could strike a bargain, perhaps"—

"What do you want for him?" asked Halvor.

"I didn't give much for him, nor is he worth much; he's a brave horse to ride, but he can't pull a cart at all; still he's strong enough to carry your knapsack and you too, turn and turn about," said the man.

At last they agreed on the price, and Halvor laid the knapsack on him, and so he walked a bit, and rode a bit, turn and turn about. At night he came to a green plain where stood a great tree, at the roots of which he sat down. There he let the horse loose, but he didn't lie down to sleep, but opened his knapsack and took a meal. At peep of day off he set again, for he could take no rest. So he rode and walked, and walked and rode the whole day through the wide wood, where there were so many green spots and glades that shone so bright and lovely between the trees. He didn't know at all where he was or whither he was going, but he gave himself no more time to rest than when his horse ate a bit of grass, and he took a snack out of his knapsack when they came to one of those green glades. So he went on walking and riding by turns, and as for the wood there seemed to be no end to it.

But at dusk the next day he saw a light gleaming away through the trees.

"Would there were folk closeby," thought Halvor, "that I might warm myself a bit and get a morsel to keep body and soul together."

When he got up to it, he saw the light came from a wretched little hut, and through the window he saw an old old couple inside. They were as grey-headed as a pair of doves, and the old wife had such a nose! why, it was so long she used it for a poker to stir the fire as she sat in front of the fireplace.

"Good evening," said Halvor.

"Good evening," said the old wife.

"But what errand can you have in coming hither?" she went on, "for no Christian folk have been here these hundred years or more."

Well, Halvor told her all about himself, and how he wanted to get to SORIA MORIA CASTLE, and asked if she knew the way thither.

"No," said the old wife, "that I don't, but see now, here comes the Moon, I'll ask her, she'll know all about it, for doesn't she shine on everything."

So when the Moon stood clear and bright over the tree-tops, the old wife went out.

"OH MOON, OH MOON!" she screamed, "can you tell me the way to SORIA MORIA CASTLE?"

"No," said the Moon, "that I can't, for the last time I shone there a cloud stood before me."

"Wait a bit still," said the old wife to Halvor, "by and by comes the West Wind; he's sure to know it, for he puffs and blows round every corner."

"Nay, nay," said the old wife when she went out again, "you don't mean to say you've got a horse too; just turn the poor beastie loose in our field and don't let him stand there and starve to death at the door."

Then she ran on—

"But won't you trade him away to me; we've got an old pair of boots here, with which you can take twenty miles at each stride; those you shall have for your horse, and so you'll get all the sooner to SORIA MORIA CASTLE."

That Halvor was willing to do at once; and the old wife was so glad at the horse, she was ready to dance and skip for joy.

"For now," she said, "I shall be able to ride to church. I too, think of that."

As for Halvor, he had no rest, and wanted to be off at once, but the old wife said there was no hurry.

"Lie down on the bench with you and sleep a bit, for we've no bed to offer you, and I'll watch and wake you when the West Wind comes."

So after a while up came the West Wind, roaring and howling along till the walls creaked and groaned again.

Out ran the old wife.

"OH WEST WIND, OH WEST WIND! Can you tell me the way to SORIA MORIA CASTLE? Here's one who wants to get thither."

"Yes, I know it very well," said the West Wind, "and now I'm just off thither to dry clothes for the wedding that's to be; if he's swift of foot he can go along with me."

Out ran Halvor.

"You'll have to stretch your legs if you mean to keep up," said the West Wind.

So off he set over field and hedge, and hill and dale, and Halvor had hard work to keep up.

"Well," said the West Wind, "now I've no time to stay with you any longer, for I've got to go away yonder and tear down a strip of spruce wood first before I go to the bleaching-ground to dry the clothes; but if you go alongside the hill you'll come to a lot of lassies standing washing clothes, and then you've not far to go to SORIA MORIA CASTLE."

In a little while Halvor came upon the lassies who stood washing, and they asked if he had seen anything of the West Wind, who was to come and dry the clothes for the wedding.

"Ay, ay, that I have," said Halvor, "he's only gone to tear down a strip of spruce wood. It'll not be long before he's here," and then he asked them the way to SORIA MORIA CASTLE.

So they put him into the right way, and when he got to the Castle it was full of folk and horses; so full it made one giddy to look at them. But Halvor was so ragged and torn from having followed the West Wind through bush and brier and bog, that he kept on one side, and wouldn't show himself till the last day when the bridal feast was to be.

So when all, as was then right and fitting, were to drink the bride and bridegroom's health and wish them luck, and when the cupbearer was to drink to them all again, both knights and squires, last of all he came in turn to Halvor. He drank their health, but let the ring which the Princess had put upon his finger as he lay by the lake fall into the glass, and told the cupbearer go and greet the bride and hand her the glass.

Then up rose the Princess from the board at once.

"Who is most worthy to have one of us," she said, "he that has set us free, or he that here sits by me as bridegroom."

Well they all said there could be but one voice and will as to that, and when Halvor heard that he wasn't long in throwing off his beggar's rags, and dressing himself as bridegroom.

"Ay, ay, here is the right one after all," said the youngest Princess as soon as she saw him, and so she tossed the other one out of the window, and held her wedding with Halvor.

Princess on the Glass Hill

ONCE ON a time there was a man who had a meadow, which lay high up on the hill-side, and in the meadow was a barn, which he had built to keep his hay in. Now, I must tell you there hadn't been much in the barn for the last year or two, for every St. John's night, when the grass stood greenest and deepest, the meadow was eaten down to the very ground the next morning, just as if a whole drove of sheep had been there feeding on it over night. This happened once, and it happened twice; so at last the man grew weary of losing his crop of hay, and said to his sons—for he had three of them, and the youngest was nicknamed Boots, of course—that now one of them must just go and sleep in the barn in the outlying field when St. John's night came, for it was too good a joke that his grass should be eaten, root and blade, this year, as it had been the last two years. So whichever of them went must keep a sharp lookout; that was what their father said.

Well, the eldest son was ready to go and watch the meadow; trust him for looking after the grass! It shouldn't be his fault if man or beast, or the fiend himself, got a blade of grass. So, when evening came, he set off to the barn, and lay down to sleep; but a little on in the night came such a clatter, and such an earthquake, that walls and roof shook, and groaned, and creaked; then up jumped the lad, and took to his heels as fast as ever he could; nor dared he once look round till he reached home; and as for the hay, why it was eaten up this year jut as it had been twice before.

The next St. John's night, the man said again it would never do to lose all the grass in the outlying field year after year in this way, so one of his sons must just trudge

72

off to watch it, and watch it well too. Well, the next oldest son was ready to try his luck, so he set off, and lay down to sleep in the barn as his brother had done before him; but as night wore on there came on a rumbling and quaking of the earth, worse even than on the last St. John's night, and when the lad heard it he got frightened, and took to his heels as though he were running a race.

Next year the turn came to Boots; but when he made ready to go, the other two began to laugh, and to make game of him, saying,—

"You're just the man to watch the hay, that you are; you who have done nothing all your life but sit in the ashes and toast yourself by the fire."

But Boots did not care a pin for their chattering, and stumped away, as evening drew on, up the hill-side to the outlying field. There he went inside the barn and lay down; but in about an hour's time the barn began to groan and creak, so that it was dreadful to hear.

"Well," said Boots to himself, "if it isn't worse than this, I can stand it well enough."

A little while after came another creak and an earthquake, so that the litter in the barn flew about the lad's ears.

"Oh!" said Boots to himself, "if it isn't worse than this, I daresay I can stand it out."

But just then came a third rumbling, and a third earthquake, so that the lad thought walls and roof were coming down on his head; but it passed off, and all was still as death about him.

"It'll come again, I'll be bound," thought Boots; but no, it did not come again; still it was and still it stayed; but after he had lain a little while he heard a noise as if a horse were standing just outside the barn-door, and cropping the grass. He stole to the door, and peeped through a chink, and there stood a horse feeding away. So big, and fat, and grand a horse, Boots had never set eyes on; by his side on the grass lay a saddle and bridle, and a full set of armour for a knight, all of brass, so bright that the light gleamed from it.

"Ho, ho!" thought the lad; "it's you, is it, that eats up our hay? I'll soon put a spoke in your wheel; just see if I don't."

So he lost no time, but took the steel out of his tinder-box, and threw it over the horse; then it had no power to stir from the spot, and became so tame that the lad could do what he liked with it. So he got on its back, and rode off with it to a place which no one knew of, and there he put up the horse. When he got home his brothers laughed, and asked how he had fared?

"You didn't lie long in the barn, even if you had the heart to go so far as the field."

"Well," said Boots, "all I can say is, I lay in the barn till the sun rose, and neither saw nor heard anything; I can't think what there was in the barn to make you both so afraid."

"A pretty story!" said his brothers; "but we'll soon see how you have watched the meadow"; so they set off; but when they reached it, there stood the grass as deep and thick as it had been over night.

Well, the next St. John's eve it was the same story over again; neither of the elder brothers dared to go out to the outlying field to watch the crop; but Boots, he had the heart to go, and everything happened just as it had happened the year before. First a clatter and an earthquake, then a greater clatter and another earthquake, and so on a third time; only this year the earthquakes were far worse than the year before. Then all at once everything was as still as death, and the lad heard how something was cropping the grass outside the barn-door, so he stole to the door, and peeped through a chink; and what do you think he saw? why, another horse standing right up against the wall, and chewing and champing with might and main. It was far finer and fatter than that which came the year before, and it had a saddle on its back, and a bridle on its neck, and a full suit of mail for a knight lay by its side, all of silver, and as grand as you would wish to see.

"Ho, ho!" said Boots to himself; "it's you that gobbles up our hay, is it? I'll soon put a spoke in your wheel," and with that he took the steel out of his tinder-box, and threw it over the horse's crest, which stood as still as a lamb. Well, the lad rode this horse, too, to the hiding-place where he kept the other one, and after that he went home.

"I suppose you'll tell us," said one of his brothers, "there's a fine crop this year too, up in the hayfield."

"Well, so there is," said Boots; and off ran the others to see, and there stood the grass thick and deep, as it was the year before; but they didn't give Boots softer words for all that.

Now, when the third St. John's eve came, the two elder still hadn't the heart to lie out in the barn and watch the grass, for they had got so scared at heart the night they lay there before, that they couldn't get over the fright; but Boots, he dared to go; and, to make a long story short, the very same thing happened this time as had happened twice before. Three earthquakes came, one after the other, each worse than the one which went before, and when the last came, the lad danced about with the shock from one barn wall to the other; and after that, all at once, it was still as death. Now when he had lain a little while he heard something tugging away at the grass outside the barn, so he stole again to the door-chink, and peeped out, and there stood a horse close outside—far, far bigger and fatter than the two he had taken before.

"Ho, ho!" said the lad to himself, "it's you, is it, that comes here eating up our hay? I'll soon stop that—I'll soon put a spoke in your wheel." So he caught up his steel and threw it over the horse's neck, and in a trice it stood as if it were nailed to the ground, and Boots could do as he pleased with it. Then he rode off with it to the hiding-place where he kept the other two, and then went home. When he got home his two brothers made game of him as they had done before, saying they could see he had watched the grass well, for he looked for all the world as if he were walking in his sleep, and many other spiteful things they said, but Boots gave no heed to them, only asking them to go and see for themselves; and when they

went, there stood the grass as fine and deep this time as
it had been twice before.

Now, you must know that the king of the country where
Boots lived had a daughter, whom he would only give to
the man who could ride up over the hill of glass, for there
was a high, high hill, all of glass, as smooth and slippery
as ice, close by the king's palace. Upon the tip-top of the
hill the king's daughter was to sit, with three golden
apples in her lap, and the man who could ride up and
carry off the three golden apples was to have half the
kingdom, and the Princess to wife. This the king had stuck
up on all the church-doors in his realm, and had given it
out in many other kingdoms besides. Now, this Princess
was so lovely that all who set eyes on her fell over head
and ears in love with her whether they would or no. So
I needn't tell you how all the princes and knights
who heard of her were eager to win her to wife, and half
the kingdom beside; and how they came riding from all
parts of the world on high prancing horses, and clad in
the grandest clothes, for there wasn't one of them who
hadn't made up his mind that he, and he alone, was to
win the Princess.

So when the day of trial came, which the king had fixed,
there was such a crowd of princes and knights under the
glass hill, that it made one's head whirl to look at them;
and every one in the country who could even crawl along
was off to the hill, for they all were eager to see the man
who was to win the Princess. So the two elder brothers
set off with the rest; but as for Boots, they said outright
he shouldn't go with them, for if they were seen with such
a dirty changeling, all begrimed with smut from cleaning
their shoes and sifting cinders in the dusthole, they said
folk would make game of them.

"Very well," said Boots, "it's all one to me. I can go
alone, and stand or fall by myself."

Now when the two brothers came to the hill of glass the
knights and princes were all hard at it, riding their horses
till they were all in a foam; but it was no good, by my

troth; for as soon as ever the horses set foot on the hill, down they slipped, and there wasn't one who could get a yard or two up; and no wonder, for the hill was as smooth as a sheet of glass, and as steep as a house-wall. But all were eager to have the Princess and half the kingdom. So they rode and slipped, and slipped and rode, and still it was the same story over again. At last all their horses were so weary that they could scarce lift a leg, and in such a sweat that the lather dripped from them, and so the knights had to give up trying any more. So the king was just thinking that he would proclaim a new trial for the next day, to see if they would have better luck, when all at once a knight came riding up on so brave a steed that no one had ever seen the like of it in his born days, and the knight had mail of brass, and the horse a brass bit in his mouth, so bright that the sunbeams shone from it. Then all the others called out to him he might just as well spare himself the trouble of riding at the hill, for it would lead to no good; but he gave no heed to them, and put his horse at the hill, and went up it like nothing for a good way, about a third of the height; and when he had got so far, he turned his horse round and rode down again. So lovely a knight the Princess thought she had never yet seen; and while he was riding, she sat and thought to herself—

"Would to heaven he might only come up, and down the other side."

And when she saw him turning back, she threw down one of the golden apples after him, and it rolled down into his shoe. But when he got to the bottom of the hill he rode off so fast that no one could tell what had become of him. That evening all the knights and princes were to go before the king, that he who had ridden so far up the hill might show the apple which the princess had thrown, but there was no one who had anything to show. One after the other they all came, but not a man of them could show the apple.

At even the brothers of Boots came home too, and had such a long story to tell about the riding up the hill.

"First of all," they said, "there was not one of the whole

lot who could get so much as a stride up; but at last came one who had a suit of brass mail, and a brass bridle and saddle, all so bright that the sun shone from them a mile off. He was a chap to ride, just! He rode a third of the way up the hill of glass, and he could easily have ridden the whole way up, if he chose; but he turned round and rode down, thinking, maybe, that was enough for once."

"Oh! I should so like to have seen him, that I should," said Boots, who sat by the fireside, and stuck his feet into the cinders as was his wont.

"Oh!" said his brothers, "you would, would you? You look fit to keep company with such high lords, nasty beast that you are, sitting there amongst the ashes."

Next day the brothers were all for setting off again, and Boots begged them this time, too, to let him go with them and see the riding; but no, they wouldn't have him at any price, he was too ugly and nasty, they said.

"Well, well!" said Boots; "if I go at all, I must go by myself. I'm not afraid."

So when the brothers got to the hill of glass, all the princes and knights began to ride again, and you may fancy they had taken care to shoe their horses sharp; but it was no good—they rode and slipped, and slipped and rode, just as they had done the day before, and there was not one who could get so far as a yard up the hill. And when they had worn out their horses, so that they could not stir a leg, they were all forced to give it up as a bad job. So the king thought he might as well proclaim that the riding should take place the day after for the last time, just to give them one chance more; but all at once it came across his mind that he might as well wait a little longer, to see if the knight in brass mail would come this day too. Well, they saw nothing of him; but all at once came one riding on a steed, far far braver and finer than that on which the knight in brass had ridden, and he had silver mail, and a silver saddle and bridle, all so bright that the sunbeams gleamed and glanced from them far away. Then the others shouted out to him again, saying he might as well hold hard, and not try to ride up the hill, for all his trouble would be thrown away; but the knight paid no heed to them, and rode straight at the hill, and right up it, till he had gone two-thirds of the way, and then he wheeled his horse round and rode down again. To tell the truth, the Princess liked him still better than the knight in brass, and she sat and wished he might only be able to come right up to the top, and down the other side; but when she saw him turning back, she threw the second apple after him, and it rolled down and fell into his shoe. But as soon as ever he had come down from the hill of glass, he rode off so fast that no one could see what became of him.

At even, when all were to go in before the king and the Princess, that he who had the golden apple might show it; in they went, one after the other, but there was no one who had any apple to show, and the two brothers, as they had done on the former day, went home and told how things had gone, and how all had ridden at the hill and none got up.

"But, last of all," they said, "came one in a silver suit, and his horse had a silver saddle and a silver bridle. He was just a chap to ride; and he got two-thirds up the hill, and then turned back. He was a fine fellow and no mistake; and the Princess threw the second gold apple to him."

"Oh!" said Boots, "I should so like to have seen him too, that I should."

"A pretty story!" they said. "Perhaps you think his coat of mail was as bright as the ashes you are always poking about, and sifting, you nasty dirty beast."

The third day everything happened as it had happened the two days before. Boots begged to go and see the sight, but the two wouldn't hear of his going with them. When they got to the hill there was no one who could get so much as a yard up it; and now all waited for the knight in silver mail, but neither saw nor heard of him. At last came one riding on a steed, so brave that no one had ever seen his match; and the knight had a suit of golden mail, and a golden saddle and bridle, so wondrous bright that the sunbeams gleamed from them a mile off. The other knights and princes could not find time to call out to him not to try his luck, for they were amazed to see how grand he was. So he rode right up the hill, and tore up it like nothing, so that the Princess hadn't even time to wish that he might get up the whole way. As soon as ever he reached the top, he took the third golden apple from the Princess' lap, and then turned his horse and rode down again. As soon as he got down, he rode off at full speed, and was out of sight in no time.

Now, when the brothers got home at even, you may fancy what long stories they told, how the riding had gone off that day; and amongst other things, they had a deal to say about the knight in golden mail.

"He just was a chap to ride!" they said; "so grand a knight isn't to be found in the wide world."

"Oh!" said Boots, "I should so like to have seen him; that I should."

"Ah!' said his brothers, "his mail shone a deal brighter than the glowing coals which you are always poking and digging at; nasty dirty beast that you are."

Next day all the knights and princes were to pass before the king and the Princess—it was too late to do so the night before, I suppose—that he who had the gold apple might bring it forth; but one came after another, first the princes, and then the knights, and still no one could show the gold apple.

"Well," said the king, "some one must have it, for it was something that we all saw with our own eyes, how a man came and rode up and bore it off."

So he commanded that every one who was in the king-dom should come up to the palace and see if they could show the apple. Well, they all came, one after another, but no one had the golden apple, and after a long time the two brothers of Boots came. They were the last of all, so the king asked them if there was no one else in the kingdom who hadn't come.

"Oh, yes," said they; "we have a brother, but he never carried off the golden apple. He hasn't stirred out of the dust-hole on any of the three days."

"Never mind that," said the king; "he may as well come up to the palace like the rest."

So Boots had to go up to the palace.

"How, now," said the king; "have you got the golden apple? Speak out!"

"Yes, I have," said Boots; "here is the first, and here is the second, and here is the third too," and with that he pulled all three golden apples out of his pocket, and at the same time threw off his sooty rags, and stood before them in his gleaming golden mail.

"Yes!" said the king; "you shall have my daughter, and half my kingdom, for you well deserve both her and it."

So they got ready for the wedding, and Boots got the Princess to wife, and there was great merry-making at the bridal feast, you may fancy, for they could all be merry though they couldn't ride up the hill of glass; and all I can say is, if they haven't left off their merry-making yet, why, they're still at it.

Shortshanks

ONCE ON a time there was a poor couple who lived in a tumble-down hut, in which there was nothing but black want, so that they hadn't a morsel to eat, nor a stick to burn. But though they had next to nothing of other things, they had God's blessing in the way of children, and every year they had another babe. Now, when this story begins, they were just looking out for a new child; and, to tell the truth, the husband was rather cross, and he was always going about grumbling and growling, and saying, "For his part, he thought one might have too many of these God's gifts." So when the time came that the babe was to be born, he went off into the wood to fetch fuel, saying, "he didn't care to stop and see the young squaller; he'd be sure to hear him soon enough, screaming for food."

Now, when her husband was well out of the house, his wife gave birth to a beautiful boy, who began to look about the room as soon as ever he came into the world.

"Oh, dear mother!" he said, "give me some of my brother's cast-off clothes, and a few days' food, and I'll go out into the world and try my luck; you have children enough as it is, that I can see."

"God help you, my son!" answered his mother; "that can never be, you are far too young yet."

But the tiny one stuck to what he said, and begged and prayed till his mother was forced to let him have a few old rags, and a little food tied up in a bundle, and off he went right merrily and manfully into the wide world. But he was scarce out of the house before his mother had another boy, and he too looked about him and said—

"Oh, dear mother! give me some of my brother's old

clothes, and a few days' food, and I'll go out into the world to find my twin-brother; you have children enough already on your hands, that I can see."

"God help you, my poor little fellow!" said his mother; "you are far too little, this will never do."

But it was no good; the tiny one begged and prayed so hard, till he got some old tattered rags and a bundle of food; and so he wandered out into the world like a man, to find his twin-brother. Now, when the younger had walked a while, he saw his brother a good bit on before him, so he called out to him to stop.

"Halloa! can't you stop? why, you lay legs to the ground as if you were running a race. But you might just as well have stayed to see your youngest brother before set you off into the world in such a hurry."

So the elder stopped and looked round; and when the younger had come up to him and told him the whole story, and how he was his brother, he went on to say—

"But let's sit down here and see what our mother has given us for food." So they sat down together, and were soon great friends.

Now when they had gone a bit farther on their way they came to a brook which ran through a green meadow, and the youngest said now the time was come to give one another names; "Since we set off in such a hurry that we hadn't time to do it at home, we may as well do it here."

"Well," said the elder, "and what shall your name be?"

"Oh!" said the younger, "my name shall be Shortshanks; and yours, what shall it be?"

"I will be called King Sturdy," answered the eldest.

So they christened each other in the brook, and went on; but when they had walked a while they came to a cross road, and agreed they should part there, and each take his own road. So they parted, but they hadn't gone half a mile before their roads met again. So they parted the second time, and took each a road; but in a little while the same thing happened, and they met again, they scarce knew how; and the same thing happened a third time also.

Then they agreed that they should each choose a quarter of the heavens, and one was to go east and the other west; but before they parted, the elder said—

"If you ever fall into misfortune or need, call three times on me, and I will come and help you; but mind you don't call on me till you are at the last pinch."

"Well," said Shortshanks, "if that's to be the rule, I don't think we shall meet again very soon."

After that they bade each other good-bye, and Short-shanks went east and King Sturdy west.

Now, you must know when Shortshanks had gone a good bit alone, he met an old, old, crook-backed hag, who had only one eye, and Shortshanks snapped it up.

"Oh! oh!" screamed the hag, "what has become of my eye?"

"What will you give me," asked Shortshanks, "if you get your eye back?"

"I'll give you a sword, and such a sword! It will put a whole army to flight, be it ever so great," answered the old woman.

"Out with it, then!" said Shortshanks.

So the old hag gave him the sword, and got her eye back again. After that Shortshanks wandered on a while, and another old, old, crook-backed hag met him who had only one eye, which Shortshanks stole before she was aware of him.

"Oh! oh! whatever has become of my eye?" screamed the hag.

"What will you give me to get your eye back?" asked Shortshanks.

"I'll give you a ship," said the woman, "which can sail over fresh water and salt water, and over high hills and deep dales."

"Well, out with it!" said Shortshanks.

So the old woman gave him a little tiny ship, no bigger than he could put in his pocket, and she got her eye back again, and they each went their way. But when he had wandered on a long, long way, he met a third time an old, old, crook-backed hag, with only one eye. This eye too,

Shortshanks stole; and when the hag screamed and made a great to-do, bawling out what had become of her eye, Shortshanks said—

"What will you give me to get back your eye?"

Then she answered—

"I'll give you the art how to brew a hundred lasts of malt at one strike."

Well, for teaching that art the old hag got back her eye, and they each went their way.

But when Shortshanks had walked a little way, he thought it might be worth while to try his ship; so he took it out of his pocket, and put first one foot into it, and then the other; and as soon as ever he set one foot into it it began to grow bigger and bigger, and by the time he set the other foot into it, it was as big as other ships that sail on the sea. Then Shortshanks said—

"Off and away, over fresh water and salt water, over high hills and deep dales, and don't stop till you come to the king's palace."

And lo! away went the ship as swiftly as a bird through the air, till it came down a little below the king's palace, and there it stopped. From the palace windows people had stood and seen Shortshanks come sailing along, and they were all so amazed that they ran down to see who it could be that came sailing in a ship through the air. But while they were running down, Shortshanks had stepped out of his ship and put it into his pocket again; for as soon as he stepped out of it, it became as small as it was when he got it from the old woman. So those who had run down from the palace saw no one but a ragged little boy standing down there by the strand. Then the king asked whence he came, but the boy said he didn't know, nor could he tell them how he had got there. There he was, and that was all they could get out of him; but he begged and prayed so prettily to get a place in the king's palace, saying, if there was nothing else for him to do he could carry in wood and water for the kitchen-maid, that their hearts were touched, and he got leave to stay there.

Now when Shortshanks came up to the palace he saw

how it was all hung with black, both outside and in, wall and roof; so he asked the kitchen-maid what all that mourning meant.

"Don't you know?" said the kitchen-maid; "I'll soon tell you: the king's daughter was promised away a long time ago to three Ogres, and next Thursday evening one of them is coming to fetch her. Ritter Red, it is true, has given out that he is man enough to set her free, but God knows if he can do it; and now you know why we are all in grief and sorrow."

So when Thursday evening came, Ritter Red led the Princess down to the strand, for there it was she was to meet the Ogre, and he was to stay by her there and watch; but he wasn't likely to do the Ogre much harm, I reckon, for as soon as ever the Princess had sat down on the strand Ritter Red climbed up into a great tree that stood there, and hid himself as well as he could among the boughs. The Princess begged and prayed him not to leave her, but Ritter Red turned a deaf ear to her, and all he said was—

"'Tis better for one to lose life than for two."

That was what Ritter Red said.

Meantime Shortshanks went to the kitchen-maid, and asked her so prettily if he mightn't go down to the strand for a bit.

"And what should take you down to the strand?" asked the kitchen-maid. "You know you've no business there."

"Oh, dear friend," said Shortshanks, "do let me go! I should so like to run down there and play a while with the other children; that I should."

"Well, well!" said the kitchen-maid, "off with you; but don't let me catch you staying there a bit over the time when the brose for supper must be set on the fire, and the roast put on the spit; and let me see, when you come back mind you bring a good armful of wood with you."

Yes, Shortshanks would mind all that; so off he ran down to the strand.

But just as he reached the spot where the Princess sat, what should come but the Ogre tearing along in his ship, so that the wind roared and howled after him. He was so tall and stout it was awful to look on him, and he had five heads of his own.

"Fire and flame!" screamed the Ogre.

"Fire and flame yourself!" said Shortshanks.

"Can you fight?" roared the Ogre.

"If I can't, I can learn," said Shortshanks.

So the Ogre struck at him with a great thick iron club which he had in his fist, and the earth and stones flew up five yards into the air after the stroke.

"My!" said Shortshanks, "that was something like a blow, but now you shall see a stroke of mine."

Then he grasped the sword he had got from the old crook-backed hag, and cut at the Ogre; and away went all his five heads flying over the sand. So when the Princess saw she was saved, she was so glad that she scarce knew what to do, and she jumped and danced for joy. "Come, lie down, and sleep a little in my lap," she said to Short-shanks, and as he slept she threw over him a tinsel robe.

Now you must know it wasn't long before Ritter Red crept down from the tree, as soon as he saw there was nothing to fear in the way, and he went up to the Princess and threatened her, until she promised to say it was he who had saved her life; for if she wouldn't say so, he said he would kill her on the spot. After that he cut out the Ogre's lungs and tongue, and wrapped them up in his handkerchief, and so led the Princess back to the palace, and whatever honours he had not before he got then, for the king did not know how to find honour enough for him, and made him sit every day on his right hand at dinner.

As for Shortshanks, he went first of all on board the Ogre's ship, and took a whole heap of gold and silver rings, as large as hoops, and trotted off with them as hard as he could to the palace. When the kitchen-maid set her eyes on all that gold and silver, she was quite scared, and asked him—

"But dear, good Shortshanks, wherever did you get all this from?" for she was rather afraid he hadn't come rightly by it.

"Oh!" answered Shortshanks, "I went home for a bit, and there I found these hoops, which had fallen off some old pails of ours, so I laid hands on them for you if you must know."

Well, when the kitchen-maid heard they were for her, she said nothing more about the matter, but thanked Shortshanks, and they were good friends again.

The next Thursday evening it was the same story over again; all were in grief and trouble, but Ritter Red said, as he had saved the Princess from one Ogre it was hard if he couldn't save her from another; and down he led her to the strand as brave as a lion. But he didn't do this Ogre much harm either, for when the time came that they looked for the Ogre he said, as he had said before—

"'Tis better one should lose life than two," and crept up into his tree again. But Shortshanks begged the kitchen-maid to let him go down to the strand for a little.

"Oh!" asked the kitchen-maid, "and what business have you down there?"

"Dear friend," said Shortshanks, "do pray let me go! I long so to run down and play a while with the other children."

Well, the kitchen-maid gave him leave to go, but he must promise to be back by the time the roast was turned, and he was to mind and bring a big bundle of wood with him. So Shortshanks had scarce got down to the strand when the Ogre came tearing along in his ship, so that the wind howled and roared around him; he was twice as big as the other Ogre, and he had ten heads on his shoulders.

"Fire and flame!" screamed the Ogre.

"Fire and flame yourself!" answered Shortshanks.

"Can you fight?" roared the Ogre.

"If I can't, I can learn," said Shortshanks.

Then the Ogre struck at him with his iron club; it was even bigger than that which the first Ogre had, and the earth and stones flew up ten yards into the air.

"My!" said Shortshanks, "that was something like a blow; now you shall see a stroke of mine." Then he grasped his sword, and cut off all the Ogre's ten heads at one blow, and sent them dancing away over the sand.

Then the Princess said again to him, "Lie down and sleep a little while on my lap"; and while Shortshanks lay there, she threw over him a silver robe. But as soon as Ritter Red marked that there was no more danger in the way he crept down from the tree, and threatened the Princess, till she was forced to give her word to say it was he who had set her free; after that he cut the lungs and tongue out of the Ogre, and wrapped them in his handkerchief, and led the Princess back to the palace. Then you may fancy what mirth and joy there was, and the king was at his wits' end to know how to show Ritter Red honour and favour enough.

This time, too, Shortshanks took a whole armful of gold and silver rings from the Ogre's ship, and when he came back to the palace the kitchen-maid clapped her hands in wonder, asking wherever he got all that gold and silver from. But Shortshanks answered that he had been home a while, and that the hoops had fallen off some old pails, so he had laid his hands on them for his friend the kitchen-maid.

So when the third Thursday evening came, everything happened as it had happened twice before; the whole palace was hung with black, and all went about mourning and weeping. But Ritter Red said he couldn't see what need they had to be so afraid; he had freed the Princess from two Ogres, and he could very well free her from a third; so he led her down to the strand, but when the time drew near for the Ogre to come up, he crept into his tree again and hid himself. The Princess begged and prayed, but it was no good, for Ritter Red said again—

"'Tis better that one should lose life than two."

That evening, too, Shortshanks begged for leave to go down to the strand.

"Oh!" said the kitchen-maid, "what should take you down there?"

But he begged and prayed so, that at last he got leave to go, only he had to promise to be back in the kitchen again when the roast was to be turned. So off he went, but he had scarce reached the strand when the Ogre came with the wind howling and roaring after him. He was much, much bigger than either of the other two, and he had fifteen heads on his shoulders.

"Fire and flame!" roared out the Ogre.

"Fire and flame yourself!" said Shortshanks.

"Can you fight?" screamed the Ogre.

"If I can't, I can learn," said Shortshanks.

"I'll soon teach you," screamed the Ogre, and struck at him with his iron club, so that the earth and stones flew up fifteen yards into the air.

"My!" said Shortshanks, "that was something like a blow; but now you shall see a stroke of mine."

As he said that, he grasped his sword, and cut off all the Ogre's fifteen heads at one blow, and sent them all dancing over the sand.

So the Princess was freed from all the Ogres, and she both blessed and thanked Shortshanks for saving her life.

"Sleep now a while on my lap," she said; and he laid his head on her lap, and while he slept she threw over him a golden robe.

"But how shall we let it be known that it is you that have saved me?" she asked, when he awoke.

"Oh, I'll soon tell you," answered Shortshanks. "When Ritter Red has led you home again, and given himself out as the man who has saved you, you know he is to have you to wife, and half the kingdom. Now, when they ask you, on your wedding-day, whom you will have to be your cup-bearer, you must say, 'I will have the ragged boy who does odd jobs in the kitchen, and carries in wood and water for the kitchen-maid.' So, when I am filling your cups, I will spill a drop on his plate, but none on yours; then he will be wroth, and give me a blow; and the same thing will happen three times. But the third time you must mind and say, 'Shame on you! to strike my heart's darling; he it is who set me free, and him will I have.'"

After that Shortshanks ran back to the palace, as he had done before; but he went first on board the Ogre's ship, and took a whole heap of gold, silver, and precious stones, and out of them he gave the kitchen-maid another great armful of gold and silver rings.

Well, as for Ritter Red, as soon as ever he saw that all risk was over he crept down from his tree, and threatened the Princess till she was forced to promise she would say it was he who had saved her. After that he led her back to the palace, and all the honour shown him before was nothing to what he got now, for the king thought of nothing else than how he might best honour the man who had saved his daughter from the three Ogres. As for his marrying her, and having half the kingdom, that was a settled thing, the king said. But when the wedding-day came, the Princess begged she might have the ragged boy, who carried in wood and water for the cook, to be her cup-bearer at the bridal-feast.

"I can't think why you should want to bring that filthy beggar boy in here," said Ritter Red; but the Princess had a will of her own, and said she would have him, and no one else, to pour out her wine; so she had her way at last. Now everything went as it had been agreed between Shortshanks and the Princess; he spilled a drop on Ritter Red's plate, but none on hers, and each time Ritter Red got wroth and struck him. At the first blow Shortshanks' rags fell off which he had worn in the kitchen; at the second the tinsel robe fell off; and at the third the silver robe; and then he stood in his golden robe, all gleaming and glittering in the light. Then the Princess said—

"Shame on you! to strike my heart's darling; he has saved me, and him will I have."

Ritter Red cursed and swore it was he who had set her free; but the king put in his word, and said—

"The man who saved my daughter must have some token to show for it."

Yes! Ritter Red had something to show, and he ran off at once after his handkerchief with the lungs and tongues in it; and Shortshanks fetched all the gold and silver and precious things he had taken out of the Ogres' ships. So each laid his tokens before the king, and the king said—

"The man who has such precious stores of gold, and silver, and diamonds, must have slain the Ogre, and spoiled his goods, for such things are not to be had elsewhere."

So Ritter Red was thrown into a pit full of snakes, and Shortshanks was to have the Princess and half the kingdom.

One day Shortshanks and the king were out walking, and Shortshanks asked the king if he hadn't any more children.

"Yes," said the king, "I had another daughter; but the Ogre has taken her away, because there was no one who could save her. Now you are going to have one daughter, but if you can set the other free, whom the Ogre has carried off, you shall have her too, with all my heart, and the other half of my kingdom."

"Well," said Shortshanks, "I may as well try; but I must have an iron cable, five hundred fathoms long, and five hundred men, and food for them to last fifteen weeks, for I have a long voyage before me."

Yes, the king said he should have them, but he was afraid there wasn't a ship in his kingdom big enough to carry such a freight.

"Oh! if that's all," said Shortshanks, "I have a ship of my own."

With that he whipped out of his pocket the ship he had got from the old hag.

The king laughed, and thought it was all a joke; but Shortshanks begged him only to give him what he asked, and he should soon see if it was a joke. So they got together what he wanted, and Shortshanks bade him put the cable on board the ship first of all; but there was no one man who could lift it, and there wasn't room for more than one at a time round the tiny ship. Then Shortshanks took hold of the cable by one end, and laid a link or two into the ship; and as he threw in the links, the ship grew bigger and bigger, till at last it got so big that there was room enough and to spare in it for the cable, and the five hundred men, and their food, and Shortshanks, and all. Then he said to the ship—

"Off and away, over fresh water and salt water, over high hill and deep dale, and don't stop till you come to where the king's daughter is." And away went the ship over land and sea, till the wind whistled after it.

So when they had sailed far, far away, the ship stood stock still in the middle of the sea.

"Ah!" said Shortshanks, "now we have got so far; but how we are to get back is another story."

Then he took the cable and tied one end of it round his waist, and said—

"Now, I must go to the bottom, but when I give the cable a good tug, and want to come up again, mind you all hoist away with a will, or your lives will be lost as well as mine"; and with these words overboard he leapt, and dived down, so that the yellow waves rose round him in an eddy.

Well, he sank and sank, and at last he came to the bottom, and there he saw a great rock rising up with a door in it, so he opened the door and went in. When he got inside, he saw another Princess, who sat and sewed, but when she saw Shortshanks, she clasped her hands together and cried out—

"Now, God be thanked! you are the first Christian man I've set eyes on since I came here."

"Very good," said Shortshanks; "but do you know I've come to fetch you?"

"Oh!" she cried, "you'll never fetch me; you'll never have that luck, for if the Ogre sees you, he'll kill you on the spot."

"I'm glad you spoke of the Ogre," said Shortshanks; "'twould be fine fun to see him; whereabouts is he?"

Then the Princess told him the Ogre was out looking for some one who could brew a hundred lasts of malt at one strike, for he was going to give a great feast, and less drink wouldn't do.

"Well! I can do that," said Shortshanks.

"Ah!" said the Princess, "if only the Ogre wasn't so hasty, I might tell him about you; but he's so cross; I'm afraid he'll tear you to pieces as soon as he comes in, without waiting to hear my story. Let me see what is to be done. Oh! I have it; just hide yourself in the side-room yonder, and let us take our chance."

Well, Shortshanks did as she told him, and he had scarce crept into the side-room before the Ogre came in.

"HUF!" said the Ogre; "what a horrid smell of Christian man's blood!"

"Yes!" said the Princess, "I know there is, for a bird flew over the house with a Christian man's bone in his bill, and let it fall down the chimney. I made all the haste I could to get it out again, but I daresay it's that you smell."

"Ah!" said the Ogre, "like enough."

Then the Princess asked the Ogre if he had laid hold of any one who could brew a hundred lasts of malt at one strike?

"No," said the Ogre, "I can't hear of any one who can do it."

"Well," she said, "a while ago, there was a chap in here who said he could do it."

"Just like you, with your wisdom!" said the Ogre; "why did you let him go away then, when you knew he was the very man I wanted?"

"Well, then, I didn't let him go," said the Princess; "but

father's temper is a little hot, so I hid him away in the side-room yonder; but if father hasn't hit upon any one, here he is."

"Well," said the Ogre, "let him come in then."

So Shortshanks came in, and the Ogre asked him if it were true that he could brew a hundred lasts of malt at a strike.

"Yes, it is," said Shortshanks.

"'Twas good luck then to lay hands on you," said the Ogre, "and now fall to work this minute; but heaven help you if you don't brew the ale strong enough."

"Oh," said Shortshanks, "never fear, it shall be stinging stuff"; and with that he began to brew without more fuss, but all at once he cried out—

"I must have more of you Ogres to help in the brewing, for these I have got ain't half strong enough."

Well, he got more—so many, that there was a whole swarm of them, and then the brewing went on bravely. Now when the sweet-wort was ready, they were all eager to taste it, you may guess; first of all the Ogre, and then all his kith and kin. But Shortshanks had brewed the wort so strong that they all fell down dead, one after another, like so many flies, as soon as they had tasted it. At last there wasn't one of them left alive but one vile old hag, who lay bed-ridden in the chimney corner.

"Oh, you poor old wretch!" said Shortshanks, "you may just as well taste the wort along with the rest."

So he went and scooped up a little from the bottom of the copper in a scoop, and gave her a drink, and so he was rid of the whole pack of them.

As he stood there and looked about him, he cast his eye on a great chest, so he took it and filled it with gold and silver; then he tied the cable round himself and the Princess and the chest, and gave it a good tug, and his men pulled them all up, safe and sound. As soon as ever Shortshanks was well up, he said to the ship—

"Off and away, over fresh water and salt water, high hill and deep dale, and don't stop till you come to the king's palace"; and straightway the ship held on her

course, so that the yellow billows foamed round her.
When the people in the palace saw the ship sailing up,
they were not slow in meeting them with songs and
music, welcoming Shortshanks with great joy; but the
gladdest of all was the king, who had now got his other
daughter back again.

But now Shortshanks was rather down-hearted, for you
must know that both the Princesses wanted to have him,
and he would have no other than the one he had first
saved, and she was the youngest. So he walked up and
down, and thought and thought what he should do to get
her, and yet do something to please her sister. Well, one
day as he was turning the thing over in his mind, it struck
him if he only had his brother King Sturdy, who was so
like him that no one could tell the one from the other, he
would give up to him the other princess and half the kingdom, for he thought one-half was quite enough.

Well, as soon as ever this came into his mind, he went
outside the palace and called on King Sturdy, but no one
came. So he called a second time a little louder, but still
no one came. Then he called out the third time "King
Sturdy!" with all his might, and there stood his brother
before him.

"Didn't I say!" he said to Shortshanks, "didn't I say you
were not to call me except in your utmost need! and here
there is not so much as a gnat to do you any harm," and
with that he gave him such a box on the ear that Shortshanks tumbled head over heels on the grass.

"Now shame on you to hit so hard!" said Shortshanks.
"First of all I won a princess and half the kingdom, and
then I won another princess and the other half of the kingdom; and now I'm thinking to give you one of the
princesses and half the kingdom. Is there any rhyme or
reason in giving me a box on the ear?"

When King Sturdy heard that, he begged his brother to
forgive him, and they were soon as good friends as ever
again.

"Now," said Shortshanks, "you know, we are so much

alike that no one can tell the one from the other; so just
change clothes with me and go into the palace; then the
princesses will think it is I that am coming in, and the one
that kisses you first you shall have for your wife, and I will
have the other for mine."

And he said this because he knew well enough that the
elder king's daughter was the stronger, and so he could
very well guess how things would go. As for King Sturdy,
he was willing enough, so he changed clothes with his
brother and went into the palace. But when he came into
the Princesses' bower they thought it was Shortshanks,
and both ran up to him to kiss him; but the elder, who was
stronger and bigger, pushed her sister on one side, and
threw her arms round King Sturdy's neck, and gave him a
kiss; and so he got her for his wife, and Shortshanks got
the younger Princess. Then they made ready for the
wedding, and you may fancy what a grand one it was,
when I tell you that the fame of it was noised abroad over
seven kingdoms.